Free

Strange
Loop

Strange Loop

Amanda Prantera

E. P. DUTTON, INC.
NEW YORK

First published in 1984 by Jonathan Cape Ltd.

Copyright © 1984 by Amanda Prantera

Published in the United States by
E. P. Dutton, Inc., 2 Park Avenue, New York, N.Y. 10016

Library of Congress Catalog Card Number: 84-72633

ISBN: 0-525-24305-4

10 9 8 7 6 5 4 3 2 1

First Edition

To Cosimo

Strange
Loop

1

It may seem ironic in view of what is to follow, but in my maturity – or perhaps I should rightly say in my old age, seeing that renown in this field is hard-earned and slow to arrive – I have become fairly well known for my theories on scientific method. Only to a very small group of people, of course, mostly doctors like myself, plus the odd therapist and researcher in other sciences; or to put it more scrupulously still, perhaps I should say to those who take a cultivated interest in the philosophical backings of their disciplines with a view to overawing less cultivated or more overworked colleagues, rather than from pure epistemic passion. I am not much read by other philosophers. Nevertheless, in this restricted and none too discriminating circle I am definitely looked on as a theoretician. Theories, in fact, in one way or another, have dogged me all my life. I had them even as a child, come to think of it, although then in the more passive sense in which one 'has' the measles or fleas: catching them from others and letting them take charge of my experience for a duration of their own choosing. A characteristic example, I remember, designed to bend both science and emotion to the shape of my own requirements (for I was like all children a serious metaphysician and needed to control both my ghosts and my machines), was on hauntings. The explanation that it offered – based I suppose on a shaky analogy to sound waves – was that exceptionally vivid or violent events remain somehow impressed on the surroundings where they have taken place, ready to be picked up by the sufficiently sensitive human receiver. Or were canine receivers also contemplated? I rather think they were. How I caught it and who from I no longer remember, nor was there anything very new or imaginative about it; but even now I can't help thinking that, however wrong, it was certainly a good theory, in that it was explanatory and adaptable and gave a very comforting account of both undesirably alarming phenomena and the equally undesirable lack of any. In its light, that is, ghosts could be seen as extant all right, but not *too* extant – much in the way that a tune is extant on a gramophone record. Dormant. A possibility. Above all, capable of being switched off.

I could, however, find no support for this particular childhood theory as I approached the house on this my second visit. Cushioned in a surround of copper beeches it spread itself proudly but relaxedly in the late sunlight like a friendly, replete and beautiful beast; and although the contrast between the pale-grey stone of the façade and the crimson of the trees should perhaps have brought back to me some echo of the terrible scene I had once witnessed there (colours often do for me the same long-distance retrieving work as smells), I was only able to register its warmth and splendour and to remember it as the one place on earth where I had been in a combination of states never again to be repeated – young and unrestrainedly in love. Why had I come back? Why had I not come back sooner? These were questions that I had become adroit in not even formulating, let alone asking or answering. Eventual answers could concern no one but myself anyway, I reasoned, for there surely *could* be no one else left to remember that summer sequence of atrocities. No one, unless, that is . . .

But here was more work for the resident censor. My stomach lurched into a familiar cramp and I waited patiently for the wave of adrenalin to subside (you would think that an experienced doctor like myself would have reacted with more physical aplomb, but no: the longer you have lived with your body and the more you know about it, the more it can disconcert you), keeping my eyes carefully averted from the upstairs windows.

'Whim. Quirk,' I thought to myself aloud, these being two of the most difficult words for me to pronounce. 'Quirky, senile stubbornness.' At any rate my colloquial English was still serviceable: indeed it was still good.

I paid off the taxi, took hold of my suitcase, and stood awkwardly in front of the high, silvery-wooden doors, trying to recall the mechanism which controlled their seemingly impregnable surface; and as I stood there – for reasons which will emerge shortly, keeping my eyes still resolutely lowered – the hitherto carefully unformulated questions jingled around in my semi-consciousness like so many keys to Bluebeard's closet, flouting censorship now that they were nearing home ground. Why are you back? Why so late? What is the use, you foolish old man? Why? Why? Why?

I had received a courteous, straightforward letter of acceptance from the present Abbess: the Convent indeed still welcomed all manner of visitors, no matter what their confession, in need of a quiet retreat for purposes of study. A distinguished scholar like myself (it was highly unlikely, I felt, that she was acquainted with my work, which a critic had once summed up clumsily but aptly as that of a 'God-is-in-his-Heaven'-is-nonsense-and-all's-hell-with-the-world philosopher) would be doubly welcome. Perhaps I should also like to note that there were now ample facilities for Congresses . . . and so forth. The signature was unfamiliar. That was only to be expected. The community I had known must be tidily laid out in symmetrical rows by now – especially if Frog-face had lived long enough to have a hand in the planning – in the miniature cemetery beyond the church. Everyone had seemed so old to me at the time: everyone except myself and . . . And? But this spot was untouch-able; I shied from it in disdain and went back to studying the doors again with practised blankness.

As I did so, a door within the door suddenly jerked open, startling me from my guarded probings, and a minute black and white figure bobbed out of it like a house-martin from its nest: a dwarf nun. A dwarf, and taking into account the tricks that hormones play with time a very old one too. Well, this one I would have remembered; but no, there had been no dwarves. Oddi-ties enough, but surely no dwarves. With deft move-ments and an exquisite smile she began wrestling with me for possession of my suitcase. I started to introduce myself but braked to an awkward halt as I recalled the rule of taxative silence which had used always to obtain at this time of day. The nun only smiled more captiva-tingly still and we continued to wrestle in silence – a transaction which did nothing to diminish my unease. Eventually, realising that I was condemned to rudeness whether I won or lost, I resigned my hold and followed her surprisingly agile progress through the wide, famil-iar corridors, forced to recognise that I must seem either very old or very imposing for an aged female midget to hold it correct to carry my luggage for me. Probably both. Old and imposing: 'Ach, so allein!' I sighed as I went (there is no language like German for sighing in), 'Und noch alt dazu.' At all events I was hard put to keep up

10

with her energetic pace, and when I fully realised just where she was leading me I moved more slowly and my breathing quickened, though not from mere exertion. We were going to the turret.

Whatever motives had led me back after so long, masochism – masochism, murkiest of motives – was among them, for I could feel myself beginning to suffer severely but with a curious readiness. Another motive of course, possibly the strongest and certainly the loftiest, despite prevailing opinion to the contrary in this dynasty of dogma under which we live, was curiosity; yet strangely I could discern no trace of it. I knew it must be there, but I could not feel even the faintest stirring and reflected that it was better so, since it was unlikely to go satisfied. With that particularly graceful capacity the English have – so often mistaken by their fellow Europeans for hypocrisy – for restoring propriety, for glazing over cracked surfaces, the whole story would doubtless by now be safely encapsulated and turned into an innocuous curiosity from the past, no more threatening than a well-dusted gibbet in a country museum. The Abbess for instance, if I told her of my previous visit, would no doubt show mild but frank interest: 'Oh! So you were here just after the war, Professor, were you? Wasn't that when there was all that unfortunate business over the Chaplain, poor man? Or was it some other priest? Such a long time ago now . . .' The voice would taper and then brighten up: 'I expect you must find things changed a great deal. But how interesting, you must remember the house as it was before we added . . .'

Yes, that was much as it would be. I would stand shivering before the dreaded closet with the blood-stained key in my hand, only to be told that there was nothing inside but musty, empty shelves. There would be no need to enter, no substance of inquiry, and my

11

disappointment would blend irreversibly with resignation and relief. I took a deep breath to steady myself after all the short, puffy ones, and followed my guide into the allotted room.

It had been furnished recently, in a near coquettish effort to cater for the worldliness of the Convent's visitors, with peony-emblazoned chintzes, sheeny tan cupboard and desk, and a crucifix formalised to the verge of unrecognisability. I relaxed slightly. There was indeed little to haunt me here. I would pass a long, quiet evening in reading – I had a couple of books with me, so there was no need to enter the library – and next morning I would return to the house of my English friends having accomplished an economical *détente* with my obsessions. If the strand of recalcitrant experience would not weave itself neatly into the fabric of my history, then at least it could be snipped off. The day after I would return to Salzburg.

But I was interrupted in my resolutions by the voice of the small pied figure, so silent up till now that I was for a moment too surprised to grasp the significance of her words. Looking me as squarely in the face as the disparity in height permitted and still smiling with authentic sweetness, she said clearly and kindly, 'Welcome back, Ludwig. I have put you in your old room as you see.' Then she spun round neatly on her heels and left the room.

So it was not until I was able to hear, beyond the noise of the words, what had actually been said that I could absorb the implications of this simple utterance; and then the crust of my memory (which had served so long to shield me from its contents) began, like a split pomegranate displaying a knobbly, tender and bruised interior, to crack open a little, to trickle over into my awareness and to demand that blandishing kind of attention which ideally only a highly trained and highly paid listener can afford to give.

I folded back the flimsy coverlet, removed my watch, my glasses and my shoes, and lowered myself painstakingly on to the narrow bed in docile surrender. I had written so often and so much on method, but now only the most banal course suggested itself to me: I must go back to the beginning, re-live that summer with chronological exactitude, and not until afterwards formulate explicitly to myself and eventually attempt to answer those questions which in the long interim I had become so adept at dodging. I must effect a kind of self-contained analysis – a rash and presumptuous undertaking perhaps, but a necessary one. Perversely, though, it was still the queries of the final stage – the half-formed whys and wherefores that capered around in my head like so many rebellious puppets – which kept rattling at me with the greater immediacy. And then there was the vexing question of the shrunken nun: how far could I rely on a memory that had just proved itself so unsound? For there *had* been no dramatically undersized nuns – of that I was quite sure. There had been, on the contrary, one very large specimen, a shy, dignified, llama-like lady whose name I never learnt, and there had been an ordinarily small French one, a Sister Zoë, who had excelled at embroidery (there was some particularly unpleasant aspect of the whole story with which she was connected, but I did not stop to examine this now). The community then, in those early post-war days before the slump in vocations had made itself felt, had been fairly well stocked: there had been a Sister Frederica and a Lobelia, and an anglicised Austrian like myself who had greeted me with fervour in dystrophic German, only to refuse to have any further contact on learning that I was interested in philosophy. 'Für Philosophie . . . ?' She had faltered, and her gaze had drifted discreetly elsewhere as if to blanket me from her own inadvertent boorishness. There had been fourteen or fifteen of them, maybe more. All however had been middle-class, middle-aged women of large to middle size. My memory was fallible, no doubt, but I was making progress. I was getting back. Perhaps it would not hurt as much as I had feared.

2

'If you are . . . well, you know. What I mean is if you are short of *money*, Vicky . . .'

Julian, the only friend I had managed to make among the English students – and not a very close one at that, I reflected, noting his embarrassment at having to mention money to me and the pop-gun emphasis with which the word finally emerged – had been the originator of the Convent plan. We were following a post-graduate course on oncology at the time, and not only was I unable to afford the fare home, if Salzburg was indeed my home any more in anything but the over-wide sense that there was still a house there in which I could stay rent-free, but I was also unable to envisage willingly settling down to earning any money in the near future. My interest in the practice of medicine had begun to pall before I had even started, and I was completing my long period of specialisation in the weary knowledge of having chosen the wrong field of study. I did however know, belatedly but not at all wearily, that a gate led out of the field, and led where I wanted to go – namely, although put like this it may sound a little stuffy, a little absurd even, towards abstraction.

'I feel also . . .' Julian was groping again laboriously for elusive synonyms. He hadn't found one when

15

discussing my finances, so I wondered how he would manage over my sex life – a subject which commanded his deferential enthusiasm.

In the works of some criminologist or other, or more likely it was a legal theorist, I once read that it is only the certainty of punishment, not its intensity or duration, which guarantees our respect for this questionable institution. This enlightened me over Julian. His respect for my powers of seduction in what had merely been a short-lived and epidermic relationship with my landlady – a bored and patient divorcee of forty-two, possessed of nothing above average except length of leg and spare time – must surely have stemmed likewise from his certainty that it had taken place. His respect – admiration even – and friendship all dated in fact from the moment that he had come round to borrow a book and had found us eloquently wedged into my inhospitable bed together; that it had been a brief, pragmatic arrangement bordering on the sordid did nothing to check these sentiments of his. He was my sworn admirer from that day on.

'I mean . . .' Cough, went Julian. Cough, scratch, twiddle. He was having a hard time and I was in no mood to soften it. 'What I mean *is*, it would be good for you to get away from this particular *place*,' he brought out at length, again with badly dosed emphasis. 'You could get down to your work properly. Wouldn't have so many distractions.'

He seemed content with this phrasing. 'Distractions, distractions, Vicky,' he repeated reprovingly, giving a racy tilt of the finger like a conductor with his baton.

'Librarian in a Convent!' I laughed. 'That means passing the whole summer surrounded by nothing but women. Mightn't that prove a bit distracting too?'

Julian's eyes widened. 'Have a heart, Vicky!' he said.

16

'They're nuns after all, hang it! Weren't you brought up a Roman Catholic? Strewth!' and he let out a delighted, sibilant breath.

All I had really been thinking of was the inevitable tedium of a summer spent cataloguing books, being polite to worthy, soda-smelling spinsters and trying to combat the apathy that always besets me when I find myself with time enough at last to dedicate to my true interests, but it would have been hard – uncharitable even – to get him to believe me.

'I'd better reconsider what I'm doing before I recommend you to my uncle for the post,' he chortled, and I grinned back at him stiffly. 'You'll have to promise, mind you, to tell me all about it afterwards.'

But as things turned out he didn't reconsider, nor did I ever tell him a word. That was the smallest courtesy I could pay him in return, for he had meant well in getting me the job, and actually did well in freeing me from the landlady, who ended up by discarding pragmatism and resorting to the none too oblique technique of parting her knees at me and growling. He even lent me his bicycle, and it was on this superb machine (how can a God exist, I sometimes think to myself conclusively, when all he could conjure up for transport was animals?) that I set off at close of term to cover the twenty-odd miles to the Convent, weighted down with one-and-a-half changes of clothes and books, books, books, all of which seemed essential to me at the moment of packing but which turned out to be so much ballast for the scant use I made of them in the end. An extension to my wardrobe would, on the other hand, have come in very handy.

I was glad Julian had not attempted to describe the place to me. He would have called it a Tudor mansion, or an Elizabethan residence, or something else parochially national and misleading, whereas in reality it was a palace, a poised and splendid palace of the high Renaissance – solid but ethereal, exalted but friendly, built in one of those rare, felicitous moments when money plus optimism does not yet add up to bad taste.

It was of palest grey stone, and the lawn, unadorned and rough-cut recently, was spread with platinum wisps of grass-cum-hay, giving off a warm, toasty smell. A disused fountain stood centrally some distance from the house, and the doors, bleached to the colour of driftwood, stood open to reveal an inner courtyard, in the very centre of which was a thin red statue.

Later on I came to notice that the statue was in fact a plaster reproduction of a red-robed, blond and bashful Christ, displaying a monogrammed heart, and that indeed in many particulars the nuns had gone about renovation with that affectionate disregard for beauty typical of the professionally religious, but my first impression, never substantially to be revised on aesthetic grounds, was one of unmarred loveliness.

A long-skirted figure padded towards me across the courtyard making elaborate gestures of welcome with one hand and emphatic ones of silence with the other. From her hissing and smiling and charade-like hand signals I understood that she was not allowed to talk and that the rule likewise applied to me. I introduced myself distinctly none the less, asked where to park my bike, and was then beckoned to follow.

The room assigned to me was situated in the north-east turret, overlooking the lawn and fountain; as far away from the sleeping-quarters of the nuns as possible. (I suspected for a moment that maybe Julian had had a word with his uncle after all.) It appeared on this first inspection that, apart from the south side of the quadrangle, fenced off from the remaining three by padded baize doors labelled uninvitingly 'Enclosure' and exclusively nun-territory, the building was uninhabited. I had been told there was a resident Chaplain, and wondered if he too was tucked away in some remote turreted recess. I wondered also – a little nervously, being constitutionally wary of the clergy – whether I would be expected to have meals with him.

The answer to this came immediately. My guide, burrowing amongst innumerable pleats, folds and pockets, produced a pencil on a long string anchored somewhere deep inside her, and a piece of crumpled but unattached paper, and scribbled down hurriedly, 'Supper with Fr. Hugh in the presbytery 7.30 sharp. You will be fetched.' She ran her thumbnail incisively under the last word: then, still smiling and hissing, withdrew. This might have been meant as an indication I was not to roam around on my own, but the message was none too explicit, so, having unpacked my few belongings and settled my books on the ample shelves where they seemed of a sudden deceptively few, I went out to scout around, discovering a conveniently close but not overly clean bathroom on the way.

I walked round the three accessible sides of the upper floor, coming up against the forbidding doors at each end. The rooms leading off the corridor were uniformly shut, and all the view I could get was a three-sided prospect of the courtyard, with its plaster Christ encircled by miscellaneous vases of cacti. There were three staircases to choose from, so I took the most impressive central ramp and completed my inspection of the downstairs lay-out, structurally similar to that above. Here, though, the doors were mostly open and without a hint of prying I was able to see a flight of communicating state rooms on either side, all sparsely furnished and bedecked with small religious pictures, numbered series of crosses, and gilt caterers' chairs. Little lacy altars, dotted about and garnished with wild flowers, completed the decorations, lending to the lofty panelled rooms a conflicting sense of void and fussiness. There was not a book to be seen anywhere.

A little disappointed by such a keen discrepancy between exterior and interior, I left the house by a small side door and found myself on a narrow shingle path which ran the length of a truly grandiose kitchen garden. Here was no taint of fussiness: everything – plants included – was large, abundant and functional. The community's entire horticultural attention had evidently been concentrated on this more utilitarian part of their territory, although it seemed but recently demoted from ornamental status, for here too a counterpart fountain stood dry, its basin piled high with rolls of wire-netting and empty seed boxes.

A short distance away a veiled figure was hoeing energetically, keeping up a low, monotonous chant synchronised to the movements of the hoe. Not wishing to seem in any way furtive, I began studiedly picking my way amongst the rows of vegetables, making for the trees which screened them from the front lawn, but I came to a standstill as the chanting left off suddenly and a bright, high-pitched speaking voice called out, 'Hello! Hello!' stretching the 'o' into a confident diphthong.

The gardening nun dropped the hoe, bundled up her skirts and fairly bounded over the neat patches, making encouraging clucking noises and what is correctly called a bee-line for me: a fiftyish but fresh and freckled frog-face beamed from under a pair of pink spectacles, set up on the brow like aviators' goggles. 'You must be the providential librarian. Well, well, well! How nice to see a young man for a change!' she said boisterously, projecting a high quantity and quality of tooth as she did so.

No doubt community living exacts sharp techniques of differentiation from those who wish to go on surviving as individuals, I thought, trying to construe her somewhat alarming approach as charitably as possible: this member had evidently chosen the characterising role of perennial tomboy. I smiled belatedly and introduced myself.

My surname must have impressed her, for she gave a sharp intake of breath and said, 'Goodness! I suppose you aren't related are you by any chance to *the* Whatsits? The ones who have their summer *Schloss* in . . . No? No. I didn't think you were. Still it's a lovely name.' She paused and then asked wistfully, 'Spelt the same?' and here at least I was able to reassure her. 'I'm sorry I interrupted your work,' I added. 'I was just trying to find my way around. The place is so large I find it a bit bewildering. I had the impression you kept a rule of silence – or am I interrupting that too?'

'No, no, no, not at all. We're not supposed to talk in the afternoons, of course, but I have a kind of dispensation, and anyway . . . ' she glanced at her watch shamefacedly ' . . . it's almost seven, so that's quite all right. Now, if you'll just let me finish off here,' this she said firmly, bossily almost, as if I had been impeding her, 'I'll take you round to church to meet the other sisters. They'll be out of benediction in a minute.'

So I waited obediently until she had come to the end of the row; then, rolling down her sleeves and dusting herself cursorily, she took my arm and piloted me through the vegetables and on to the lawn and across the front of the house, plying me with dates and a stream of unsolicited architectural information, delivered with the condensed rapidity of a bulletin for tourists. I did my best to take it all in, being always a conscientious visitor to stately houses, but as we passed the far turret – the twin to my own – my attention was caught by a brusque

21

movement at the window, as if someone had been lean-
ing out and then drawn back from it hurriedly. Frogface
lowered her pink glasses abruptly and peered at me with
what amounted to downright crossness, making me feel
for a moment slightly uneasy. Had I committed some
kind of gaffe, I wondered.

Surely there could be nothing wrong in looking up at a
window from this chastely acute angle? Had there been
something or someone there I shouldn't have noticed?
Or was she merely offended by my inattentiveness? To
cover up I mumbled some inane comment on the profusion of Virginia creeper and this seemed to placate her,
as she said, beaming once more, 'It's a pity you won't be
here to see it in the autumn. Reverend Mother is always
on at me to clip it back, but I quote her "The Lord giveth
and the Lord taketh away" and she hasn't come up with
a suitable counter-quote yet.' She gave a triumphant,
equine snort of laughter.

I could have suggested one myself, but refrained. To
ensure a maximum of tranquillity and time I wanted to be
neither disliked nor liked: a state of equilibrium which I
have sought many times since, and I think – except in
the one fell case with which this story is concerned –
strenuously achieved. The nature of my gaffe did not
return to perplex me until later that evening.

The church, a small building half-hidden by the curv-
ing colonnade of beeches, turned out to be a converted
mock-Tudor games pavilion, almost totally encased in
white roses. Frogface pointed out to me the Chaplain's
cottage near by, rose-covered in rival profusion, and
beyond it a block of beautifully mellowed stables
crowned by a sundial. Further off still, there was a much
overgrown pond and a contrastingly bald and hum-
mocky plot which was their cemetery. Despite its all
being pointed out to me with such genuine pride, I

gained the overall impression of a claustrophobic micro-cosm, and this was reinforced by the sight of a high stone wall, badly dilapidated in places but seemingly unscal-able, encircling the entire property. Behind the clang of the nun's brisk voice there was little to be heard except for a faint accompaniment of whirrings and rustlings from the pond until a bell from the church began to ring, shaking the small building and its masses of roses in disproportionate rhythm, and a file of black and white figures followed by a cluster of grey ones began to troop sedately out along the flagstone path, rosaries jangling, strong boots thumping, fingers dripping holy water. There was a burst of subdued chatter; the line broke and the leading figure – a frail, erect woman with the scatty eyes of a hare – came quickly forward with her hand outstretched.

'Reverend Mother,' whispered Frogface at my elbow in tones of patently feigned awe, 'you may kiss her hand, you know,' and I saw her mouth pleat with satisfaction as I shook the proffered hand neutrally instead.

'Dear Doctor,' began the Abbess, holding my hand in a cool, silky grasp and focusing her errant gaze some-where between my hairline and the trees behind, 'I see you have already met up with our invaluable Sister Lucy. Sister, I hope you have shown the Doctor round and made him welcome?'

We both smiled assent. The voice was thin and fati-gued – like the eyes, merely grazing its target – and did not invite a verbal reply.

I noted that its owner fitted neatly into my theory on personality conservation, in having adopted a character-ising role of absent-minded sanctity; perhaps her exalted position resulted directly from this, for there was little of the leader in her make-up, and it became clear to me later how much decisional power rested instead in the earth-stained and apparently humbler hands of her vigorous subordinate. She made a faint looping gesture with her forearm, which served as a general introduction to the rest of the community, and curious faces gathered round me in a chequered ring, smiling various degrees of welcome. It has always been my habit to refer to people privately by nicknames – usually rather unimaginative ones, I confess, since I rely on them as a purely mnemonic device – and so to Frogface and Popeye I mentally added Whiskers, Lockjaw, Pinhead (this was the tall one), Simper and Wallaby (this for my compatriot, who moved from place to place with a terrific bundling of the haunches, her hands held limply before her like the paws of a begging dog). Ah, yes, and Jaundice. The only other two subsequently to earn classification for characteristics not immediately noticeable were Rumble and – for some by now untraceable reason – Coot. I politely answered all their questions, and grinned and grinned back at them until my teeth grew chilly.

I was beginning to discover that a degree in medicine brings heavy disadvantages in its wake in that it tends to dismantle certain social and cultural barriers which for a man of my temper and inclinations would have come in very useful. A one-sided intimacy is sometimes alarmingly rapidly established, especially by women, and I have met several who as an opening gambit go so far as to bare parts of the body to me to point out some infirmity or other. If only they realised how irksome I find it – not so much the denuding as the underlying assumption that the revealed warts, pimples, nodules, swellings and so forth possess intrinsic power to enthral, and that in letting me in on them they are in fact generously granting me a kind of treat. At that time, though, I was sufficiently fresh from medical school to find this kind of approach almost flattering (let me hasten to add that the nuns' version was a particularly restrained one); and I stood my ground patiently, dispensing attention and advice on minor matters, not losing grip on my audience until I happened to counsel for someone's sore throat a brand of suppository. There was a moment's silence, during which the word continued to rebound in all its audacity, then of one accord the group began to break up and to wander towards the house. The Abbess's fugitive eye met mine directly for the first, and, as far as I can recall, last time, in querulous distaste, and I found myself alone again with Sister Lucy.

'Not to worry, not to worry,' she said, stroking my sleeve with a grubby index finger. 'Residues of puritanism.' Then prodding the finger more companionably still into my ribcage, 'You wicked old Mittel-Europeans, now. You have a much healthier attitude towards the flesh.'

As she spoke she began propelling me once more along the path. 'I'm taking you over to our Chaplain, Father Hugh, who has very kindly put his house at your disposal for supper,' she explained as we went. 'We nuns eat on our own, of course – puritanism again wouldn't you think? – and he was afraid you'd get a bit lonely in the evenings. You won't mind lunch on a tray, though, will you?'

My concurrence must have been only too plain, for she added straight away, 'I thought not. Supper was Father's own idea. Truth of the matter is, I think he gets a little lonely himself. Lonely, or overwomaned!' she finished debonairly, and having pushed open the door and called out 'Father! Father Hugh!' very loudly indeed, getting no answer, she gave me yet another friendly tap on the arm and scampered away humming to herself the opening bars of a Strauss waltz.

This was the first of many suppers with Jitters. Beyond convenience, it was – as Frogface had guessed – loneliness and only loneliness that drew us together thus, evening after evening. I have never before nor since spent, I think, so much time alone with a man of tastes, opinions and experience so widely divergent from my own (I was never in the army, and my father died before I was born, which rules out two fertile opportunities for this), yet there we sat night after night, talking earnestly to one another on subjects as revealing and engaging as only the intensely personal or intensely general can be. I got to look forward even to these evening discussions, in spite of the fact that this ignorant, muddle-headed, superstitious little monk was no dialectical match for me. Mostly we discussed religion, of course, or more properly the philosophy of religion and meta-religion, and I would take an almost cruel pleasure in hammering into him the wherefores of my disbelief, whilst he would keep filling up my glass, plying me with cigarettes, and emitting frequent, almost happy sighs. Each time I cornered him in argument he would lift up his nervous little hands, shake them at me as if trying to scare away a bird, and splutter, 'Well! Well, now! Is there no limit to what I must sit and listen to?' and sometimes would leave the room, flapping in fury. But then he would be back with more beer, and would start all over again, trying to discover some chink in my rational armour, usually resorting in desperation to rhetorical questions on the lines of, 'But when you see the sun rise, Wiggie,' (he had asked me what my friends called me, but could no more manage the androgynous 'Vicky' than I could the distressing 'Father') 'don't you ever feel there *must* . . . ?' or, 'Have you never been in *love* then, Wiggie?' and, 'When you're listening to your Mozart, now . . . ?' Then I would know it was time to go, for his lack of cogency in argument used really to rile me, and I would traipse back to my turret, angry at having wasted yet another evening that I could have devoted more profitably to study or even to light reading, yet knowing that the very next evening I would be back there again and delighted to be so. Of course, when it came to the crunch Hugh deserted me entirely – it was no accident that I baptised him Jitters – but I never really held this against him.

That first evening, though, he began by questioning me in a perfunctory and stilted way about my background and general outlook, as if he had been officially commissioned to do so (as was indeed probably the case); at any rate he showed no personal interest in my replies until we broached the topic of my religious beliefs. Even then, although his habitual nervousness increased and his fingers danced up and down on his knees in a frenetic, silent sonata, he seemed intent not so much on the content of my answer as on its falling within an acceptable limit, and he prefaced each question by laying down for the purpose an almost visible set of tramlines. I realised that he must be particularly anxious for some reason that I should pass muster, but at the time I could only put it down to his desire for company: as Frogface had observed, he probably felt himself over-womaned. Anyway his anxiety won me over in part, and on that occasion I kept tidily inside the tramlines, left my atheism unaired, and was rewarded by an uncharacteristically relaxed smile.

Our supper was trundled across by one of the grey-clad serving nuns, whose function, Jitters explained to me as if it were a self-evident and necessary state of affairs, was to free their more exalted sisters from distracting, material tasks and thus indirectly increase the volume of prayer directed daily heavenwards. These evanescent members of the community were relegated

27

both figuratively and literally to the back pews, and I was never granted a formal introduction to any of them as far as I can remember. After a while I began hardly to notice them any more, which may have been discreditable of me but was not entirely my fault, since the ban on conversation seemed to apply to them at all times and my greetings were invariably met by nothing more encouraging than variations on the hissing and smiling theme.

The meal which arrived – I cite it merely as a representative example – wheeled forcefully but expressionlessly by one of these creatures over the humpy terrain, consisted in corned beef, crackers, badly washed salad and two bars of chocolate. We sat outside in deckchairs to eat it, the examination over, and chatted easily on less taxing matters such as where to dry socks and obtain tobacco.

My host did not speak much of the Convent or of his life and work there, except to mention that he had been farmed out by his own order to fill the post of resident Chaplain on health grounds, (by the way he said it he might have been serving a life-sentence); nor, although he well knew that I was a doctor and he himself a seriously sick man, did he then – or ever, as far as I remember – talk to me about his health. This restraint drew from me a first feeling of respect on which the subsequent one of tenuous friendship was based. Poor little Hugh, caught up in matters so much bigger than he could cope with. Poor pusillanimous little personality, housed within such a rickety frame. Small wonder that there was nothing there for me to lean on. As we sat on into the loitering summer darkness, listening to the stirring of the trees and making, for this once, detached and polite conversation on the perfectly humdrum subjects I have mentioned, and just as I was about to take myself off to bed early, having been as yet issued with no key of my own, a small incident took place – insignificant at the time, but in retrospect summing up with beautiful, random precision the whole arc of our relationship. A bat, flying towards us from the front of the house, shone coloured for a second between the trees, as if it had crossed a shaft of light. For the second time that day I received a faint impression that the room in the other turret was inhabited.

'Does anyone besides myself sleep on the north side?' I asked unconcernedly, giving my legs a good stretch before getting to my feet.

In simultaneous answer the monk's hands shot up in alarm (whether at the question or at the incident was impossible to tell), and there came a sharp rending noise as the canvas of the deckchair gave beneath my weight. I sat helpless, ensconced within the frame, while he danced about in front of me twittering with laughter and giving ineffectual tugs at my sleeve. 'I *knew* that would happen one of these days. I knew it. I knew it. Nothing gets done here until it's too late,' he managed to say composedly between onslaughts of nervous giggles. I dragged myself out angrily, aware of a searing pain in the rectum and a scarcely less painful loss of dignity; and there it all was in a nutshell – a small-scale prefiguration of future events: the awkward, unanswered question, the ungainly fall, unmentionable pain, and the little priest dithering around on the side-lines in his role of convulsed and helpless spectator. Except, of course, that the analogous pain was not located in my rectum – would that it had been – and Hugh was no longer convulsed by mirth but by a much less palatable emotion.

I slept that night on my stomach on account of the bruise, ejaculated as I always do – no, let me correct myself: as I always used to do – when in that position, and spent the early hours of the morning trying to restore the convent sheets to their former purity. I suppose this too can be read as fitting into the premonitory nutshell.

From that morning on, my days began to assume pattern and rhythm. Imposed from without came the punctual tollings of the bell calling the nuns to their frequent and regular orations, followed by the sweep of skirts and thunder of hefty shoes in obedience to its call; the daily deliveries of mail and groceries accompanied by the shrill, excited cries of Coot the Sister Bursar (here perhaps lies the clue to her name's etymology) whose ability to deal advantageously with tradespeople was legendary amongst her companions; and the cadence of my meals, which I began to note with pleasure respected that of the days of the week, the only divergence being that corned beef cropped up twice – on Wednesdays and Sundays. To this already consoling and inspiring struc- ture – I have always found regularity and predicta- bility two necessary working conditions if one is to produce innovative and unpredictable ideas, and cite as an example to unpunctual students the unwavering precision of the trim little philosopher from Königsberg; although, as my brighter unpunctual students are quick to note, this hackneyed example supports my theory not one whit – I added the regularities of my own personal timetable.

I devoted each morning from nine till one to my task in the library. There had been no stipulation of working hours, but however anxious I was to have plenty of spare time in which to pursue my own interests – meaning, of course, my studies in scientific methodology; not the very different interests which I actually ended up in pursuing – four hours seemed to me a diligent quota. After lunch I would brew up a clandestine cup of coffee on the minuscule spirit stove I had brought with me (at least I thought of it as coffee, although it was in fact some kind of wartime surrogate made from fig seeds – far more difficult to come by, you would have thought – which a relative continued to send me from Austria and to which I had become perversely addicted), would smoke a cigarette or two and then settle down to a couple of hours' study. From four to five I would walk to the village, or substitute for the walk gymnastics in case of rain, and lastly put in another hour or so's work in the evenings to replace returned volumes and tidy things up generally, ready for a fresh start on the following day. Oh yes, I am methodical all right, or was, at least, until extraneous factors began to upset my schedule.

The library itself, which had escaped my first perusal owing to the fact that it was kept rigorously closed at all times for fear of dust and the door only opened to a cautious minimum for strict purposes of exit and entry, had also and fortunately escaped renovation. It was a long, wide, generously proportioned room, well lit both naturally and artificially, its every available wall space given over to book storage. Despite the huge variety of colours which must in fact have gone into their make-up the walls gave off a homogeneous aura of pale golden-brown, at midday amounting almost to amber. Centuries of respectful polishing had lent them too a warm, waxy smell which seemed somehow to match the colouring.

My desk there was wide and accommodating, the chair comfortable; the ladders ran smoothly, and the silence had a less imposed feel about it. You would have thought I should find it an inviting place to work in – much better than my poky little turret where the windows were heavily leaded and narrow and the light bulb was of the 25-watt denomination to be found throughout the entire convent with the exception of the library and the church – but it had withal that public, open feel about it that libraries always do; my desk, despite its comfort, was vulnerably central, and at any moment one was liable to hear the creaky, self-conscious footfall of one of the heavily shod ladies, nosing around for reading matter or, more disconcertingly still, just nosing around. I was happier therefore studying in the turret. Happier, and also busier, for besides my book work I was very gradually becoming engaged in a second activity: fitful observation of the other turret. There had been as yet no more lights from it, but the window on my side more often than not stood open, particularly at night, and now and again I thought I could see little movements in the room beyond.

From this it seems a natural step to deduce that I was bored, for there was as yet no reason – apart from Jitters's possible alarm at my questioning and Frogface's frown when first I had glanced at the window – for my finding the turret of particular interest, but this was not so. As a matter of fact I found my cataloguing work positively congenial, since it entailed imposing order, both criterial and logistic, and I managed to make it entail physical exercise as well by transferring all the volumes by hand, and by scaling the ladders using my arms only when I was in there unobserved.

Apart from the mere fact of their presence the reading nuns were no bother to me directly, since they helped themselves from a shelf containing devotional works, and even from this already limited selection they seemed to favour only a part: a dozen or so books were in constant rotation and one in particular – a slim volume of meditations by a, to me, unheard-of author – would hardly be set on my desk by one pair of hands than another would rapaciously claim it.

The bulk of the collection, theirs by the incidental fact

of its having come into their possession with the house itself, had little to do with the nuns and still less with their religion. There were a number of geographical works, travel books – mediocre but many and voluminous – dictionaries, encyclopaedias, atlases, tome after tome on medicine and astronomy, beside many particularly fine botanical volumes. The bents of the mind, or minds rather, which had amassed this collection – a remarkable one in size and scope for the home of an otherwise unremarkable English country family – had evidently been wholly scientific. The closest thing to fiction I came across was Rousseau's *Émile*. The collection also incorporated quite a number of philosophical classics, although this I did not in fact discover until my third evening when I found, lying on my table ready to be put back into place, a small pile of leather-bound volumes, plainly not from the overworked shelf: Marcus Aurelius, Epicurus – both in translation – and some seminal treatise of British empiricism; I think it was Locke's celebrated essay. Using the system of classification which I had come to supplant, I found their shelf of origin and discovered there a sizeable hoard of staple philosophical works tucked away in a high, remote corner. I noticed too that, though the higher regions were habitually dusty, being overlooked evidently by an otherwise diligent early-morning cleaner, most of these volumes were dust-free and many had been lightly scored in pencil; comments had been written in the margins and then imperfectly erased, leaving little flakings of india rubber amongst the pages.

I felt a surge of excitement and irritation mixed: there was another amateur philosopher abroad. Was this a good thing or a bad? A potential fount of amusement, embarrassment, or boredom? It all depended on who it was, of course, and then equally heavily on the reason for their interest: it might merely turn out to be Father Hugh, rubbing shoulders with dangerous freethinkers the stronger to confirm his own fey superstitions; or it might be my compatriot, founding her unwavering disapproval on conversance rather than prejudice. In the light of these considerations I decided to try and find out more about this voracious reader who shared my disreputable taste for philosophy.

The next day therefore, instead of repairing to my turret after lunch to wrestle with that porcupine problem which is the mathematical quantification of clinical judgment and on which my notes had got no further than the feeble mapping of 'Well,' 'Fair,' 'Poor,' and 'Seriously ill' on to values 1, 2, 3 and 4 (or perhaps the other way round, so as to shade down to 0 for 'dead'), I returned to my desk in the library to try to identify my quarry.

Whether it was the silence and the warmth of the gentle mote-bespecked shaft of light which fell across the desk, or whether it was the lack of a good, strong cup of fig-seed coffee and my afterlunch cigarette, anyway for some reason I must have dozed off for a while, for the next thing I was aware of was the heavy clump and swish of a booted and skirted individual closing the library door behind her and stomping rapidly away down the corridor. A two-volume edition of Hume's *Inquiry* lay neatly on the desk before me and the ladder stood directly beneath the pertinent shelf.

I hurried to the door, just in time to see one of the nuns – which one I could not tell – tackle the corner staircase at high speed, a small pile of books under her arm.

So it was one of the nuns. Aha! I felt almost as if I had made a telling discovery, although all that I had in fact accomplished was the elimination of the Chaplain, and he had never really figured with me as a viable suspect. The next day or so would tell me more. I resolved to suspend my afternoon studies for a while and remain vigilant.

I returned to my desk, and began to leaf through the bitterly logical Hume – one of the thinkers I feel really friendly towards. Ha! Madame had been doing a lot of scribbling, I noticed. She had also been more than usually careless over her erasings. I held the book to the light and then horizontal to my nose. The pencil had made quite an impression. I could make out squiggles and signs, as if someone had been doing arithmetic – no, not arithmetic; it looked more like . . . but surely it couldn't . . . ? Yes, yes, no doubt about it, it was symbolic logic – in the Polish notation. My interest began to grow. No matter what had been written the mere fact that the reader was familiar with such a technique was in itself proof of a fairly sophisticated philosophical *savoir-faire*. I began systematically to comb through both volumes, page by page. Nowhere did I find anything both integral and legible however until I reached the very last page where, pencilled clearly and doubtless overlooked, stood the perspicacious comment – perhaps a trifle flippant, but certainly perspicacious, 'But yours is a causal argument, Mr Hume!' The word 'argument' was underlined, and at the very bottom of the page, quite unaccountably, was the drawing of a koala bear in tears.

As the Chaplain and I sat over our after-dinner beer together that evening, huddled under blankets since the night was chilly (faintly high-smelling, stiff ones that must have belonged originally in the stables), and were getting into one of what were fast on the way to becoming our habitual metaphysical arguments-cum-conversations, I mentioned to him my detection of the philosopher nun.

'Nonsense!' he replied abruptly, slopping some beer

on to the blanket. 'What ever will you think of next, Wiggie!' And then, as I held to my thesis and told him how I had only just missed identifying the nun who had returned the books and intended to catch her at it the next time and speak to her outright, he said earnestly and quickly, 'I wouldn't do that, Wig. No, I wouldn't do that if I were you. Maybe she does have a taste for these readings, but it's a delicate matter, you know, in a religious set-up like this. No, honestly, I wouldn't say anything to her about it. Might embarrass the poor thing. The best thing is to keep quiet. Now, can I rely on you to do just that?' The voice was even more anxious than usual and I realised that without in the least meaning to I had succeeded in upsetting him greatly. The little, nut-coloured eyes peered at me pleadingly, squinting with worry.

'Then I won't speak to her of philosophy, that I promise,' I assured him, using a crafty formulation which I felt left me quite free to accost the lady on the related but quite distinct subject of symbolic logic.

'You're a good lad, Wig,' said Jitters feelingly, blowing into his beer and taking a good swig, 'and it'll be doubly good of you to ask me as few questions as possible – the less questions asked in this rum place the better.' Then, as if aware of having been betrayed into overemphasis, 'No need for promises, though, nothing like that. Don't needle the poor creature, that's all.'

It was probably then, and thanks in part to this momentary lifting of the curtain of propriety in referring to the Convent as a 'rum place', that I began to notice that the Chaplain – besides being a sick man on purely physical grounds – was also psychologically ailing. His complaint I could only diagnose as fear, although there are of course a lot of less uncompromising ways of labelling it. Hence the jitters, and hence the nickname.

Not that he manifested this fear in any particularly dramatic way, but he had about him that air of dull, persistent and intense unhappiness that only those who live so close and so aligned to fear that they can neither isolate it nor combat it, acquire. I had had occasion to note it in survivors from concentration camps, in victims of school bullying, and in inmates of lunatic asylums, but I had never before seen it in a free adult, living a life of his own choosing, untrammelled by the dictates of an institution. I reckoned it must be due to his illness, about which he was so reticent, and that his distaste for the Convent – and as I gradually discovered for the majority of its inhabitants – must stem mainly from the contingent fact that it was probably his last, reluctant appointment. But about this, as about so many other things, I was entirely mistaken. The diagnosis alone was correct.

The next book missing from the philosophical section was Kant's most celebrated *Critique*, so I was not surprised to see day after day elapse without any sign of it returning. I kept vigil punctually each afternoon, however, except for one occasion when Frogface conscripted me for bean-picking with such overpowering decision that I could in no way refuse; it was a minor matter – a basketful of beans on one side, a little amateur detectives on the other – but as I began politely to decline the offer and she just as politely and jestingly to insist I accept, I was given a taste of the adamantine nature of her will. I told myself that I was giving in out of a desire to remain within the bounds of civility, and she had evidently banked on my doing just this, but had I transgressed these bounds I had the feeling that she would have tackled me there – on the terrain of explicit rudeness – just as gladly and just as successfully. A tough nut, Sister Lucy. Anyway, when I had finished picking the wretched things, my own considerable will still smarting from this token clash and token defeat, I hurried back to the library to find the place on the upmost shelf still vacant. Luckily Kant is another tough nut. Two more afternoons and still no return. On the third, no Kant, but an interesting episode none the less: the much-sought-after little book of meditations came briefly home to roost, and was pounced on this time not by two hands but by four. A tussle and a squabble resulted, right there in the library – reign of silence at all times – and to make matters worse during the afternoon curfew. I do not know what punishment, if any, the two offenders received, but Sister Zoë, the embroideress, went around with a red, blotchy face for nearly a week. It was thus that I came to appreciate the appeal of the volume though, for in the thick of the struggle Sister Zoë cried out, 'But I *promised* Father Constantine I would read it. What am I to tell him when he comes back? This is too bad. Mon Dieu, mon Dieu!' and resorting to her native French she began bemoaning her predicament, her neat, roseate fingers keeping a tight hold of the prize.

'Father is not due for a good while yet. There's plenty of time for you to read it. And I was next on the list. I'm sorry, but that's only fair, Sister,' countered her opponent, her eyebrows disappearing behind the starched wimple in the exertion.

I coughed loudly, and benefiting from a lull in the tussle took the book from them. It was wafer thin and printed large – surely a couple of hours would suffice even for the most thorough perusal. 'I think your colleague is right,' I began awkwardly – 'colleague' sounded quite medical and wrong – 'if her name is on the list . . .' and I made a show of consulting the papers before me.

'There is no list!' interrupted the French nun huffily.

'There may be no list but there was a spoken agreement,' said the other. 'I suppose that means nothing to you!'

I glanced again at the flimsy object of such contention. The title, printed in inopportunely lush golden lettering, ran, *With this Ring: Prayers to Christ the Bridegroom*, and underneath in letters of equal size and opulence, 'Constantine Read', followed by a spate of punctuated capitals denoting goodness knows what. I just had time to glimpse the opening line of the first prayer which began chattily and probably only too aptly for most readers, 'Lord, I have had a bad week . . . ' when the book was snatched from me by the more robust and righteous English nun – I think it was Rumble – who stuffed it determinedly into the recesses of her capacious habit.

There the episode ended, but I had learnt the secret of the book's popularity amongst the community members: not only was the theme itself emotionally stimulating, but the manner of presentation confidential, bordering on the saucy; added to which its author was shortly to arrive in person.

'Who is this Constantine Read?' I asked Sister Zoë, who was half-heartedly rummaging about in the divinity shelf for a substitute.

'Ssssh!' she whispered back, hypocritically reminding me of the rule of silence. Then her eyes took on an oneiric shine, 'A great man,' she murmured, purring out the r's, 'a grreat man and a grreat prriest.'

'Hmph!' I grunted to myself, unconvinced, and determined to seek the more balanced opinion of Jitters on this point.

The very next afternoon the *Critique* returned to base. I was disconcerted to see that the bearer was Whiskers, but summoning up my courage, and quoting to myself

Aristotle's reminder that even the most unprepossessing amongst us may be a valuable philosophical mouthpiece, I smiled at her encouragingly and showed her a slip of paper on which I had written a few samples of symbolised arguments, expressed of course in the Polish notation – I had had to check this in one of my textbooks for it was a method with which I was not familiar. 'I came across this on my desk here this morning,' I whispered across to her, as casually as that form of heightened communication would allow. 'Any idea what it means?'

Whiskers took the note and held it close to her nose, studying it obligingly. Her face remained blank.

'Humph. Looks like maths to me,' she whispered back noncommittally. 'Maybe carpenter's measurements or something. Shouldn't worry – looks just a scrawl.' And she lumbered off towards the ladder in search of further reading – two commentaries on the *Critique* this time. As I recorded the titles I searched in my mind for some other opening which would confirm my suspicions without violating my promise to Father Hugh, although I was pretty sure that her ignorance was genuine. Perhaps I had been observing her too intently though, for slowly a shrewd look began to appear through the bristles, and she reached out for the slip of paper which I had left lying on the desk.

'I think I'll keep that if you don't mind,' she said ponderously and aloud. But acting quickly I slid the paper from under her grasp and crumpled it into a ball, keeping my fist tight around it. This had her defeated, and unwilling to evince further interest, she said officiously, 'If I were you I should hand that in to Reverend Mother. It may be important after all. You never know.'

I gave her a silly smile. I knew now that this was not

my clandestine commentator. She was procuring the books for someone else. But for whom? Furthermore, if the Reverend Mother was aware of this traffic, then why did not whoever it was come in person to make a choice of reading matter? Could it be that there was an invalid closeted away somewhere – a nun perhaps, or a guest of the Convent? Could it not be, as I already heavily suspected, the mysterious inhabitant of the other turret? I determined to keep a closer watch on the window from now on.

For two nights running I left Jitters's table early with the excuse of not feeling well, and, sitting in the dark of my own turret, I saw an electric light go on and off in the corresponding window exactly seven times. The window was pushed open twice, and on the second night, which was a very warm one, it remained open. Once a duster was shaken out, or a rag of some kind; and in the depths of both nights a faint yellowish glow was noticeable, as if from a night-light or candle. There was no doubt about it – a mere two nights' observation was sufficient to go by – the turret was inhabited. I was equally sure that it was inhabited by my philosopher, whom I had begun to picture as male, and either bedridden or very old (the ludicrous, crying koala suggested a possible sufferer from arterial sclerosis), and as desirous moreover for an opportunity for philosophical discussion with me – if only I could somehow manage to contact him. It was only guesswork of course at this stage that I was indulging in, and guesswork frivolously undertaken out of reluctance to get to grips seriously with my studies, but I already had a distinct feeling, however slender the evidence on which it was based, that contact would be hard to make. There was something secretive about the whole thing, I felt sure; something I was not supposed to know; something which, if I used the official channels for this purpose, I would actually be prevented from knowing.

It was therefore out of a sense of abstract commitment to straightforwardness that I chose the semi-official channel of Father Hugh and told him outright about my conviction that the turret was lived in, and about my intention of getting in touch with its inhabitant.

We were sitting inside the house that particular evening, taking shelter from an intermittent drizzle but still wedged into the precariously mended deckchairs, for the nuns had furnished their Chaplain's abode in an almost offensively threadbare fashion and these were the only comfortable seats available. We sat facing one another across a dusty, empty hearth, and the light from the wobbly, parchment-shaded standard lamp fell slantwise on to the monk's face, giving me ample opportunity to observe his reactions. I was beginning to find them rather interesting.

This time he used no deviating tactics; there was no rending of canvas either, and he showed no strong emotion. More than anything he seemed relieved at my certainty, as if it took the matter quite out of his hands, and he looked at me calmly, in open resignation. 'You're right of course, Wig. There is someone up there. Some Polish refugee or other. Or maybe Hungarian. I don't really . . . '

'Das stimmt!' I broke in, mixing my languages in the excitement. 'Then it is my philosopher?'

Jitters splayed his hands in front of his face and was silent for a moment as if in intense concentration, his eyes tight shut. 'I don't know for sure,' he said tensely, 'I'm not in . . . You see the thing is I don't have much dealings with . . . The fact is . . . ' Here his voice dropped as if he had completed the sentence and he reverted to concentration behind the grille of his fingers. I was unwilling to interrupt, for fear of drying him up altogether, but my fear was unnecessary; he dried himself up, and sharply. Giving a weak little shake of the head, he said, 'I'm sorry, Wiggie. I'm truly sorry, but I can't give you a straight answer. In fact I can't really give you an answer at all. I've asked you before, and I'm asking you again. I know you're a mature, clever chap and I know I can trust you, so can I have your word for it now that you'll leave the matter be? There's no secret about the whole thing. This . . . ' He hesitated. ' . . . person is regularly in the nuns' charge, and if they are, well . . . discreet about it, it's because they have their reasons. It's a sad case; a very sad case indeed. War and things, you know.'

His voice had become sad too as he said this, again with his usual brand of fear-engendered sadness. It made me unwilling to press him further, and I think he was so relieved by my lack of insistence that he forgot to exact from me the pledge he had asked for. This was an important oversight. I am indeed trustworthy, but I am also very precise in my use of terms. I had made no promises this time and given no word.

With a clear conscience therefore – or at least sufficiently so – I pursued my inquiry. My next step was a risky one, and taken on impulse. Right under Whiskers's nose as she collected yet another tome for her voracious, mysterious client, I scribbled the following message on the fly-leaf: '($\exists$x) (Px·Lx) where P=is a philosopher, L=is lonely' – the meaning being roughly, 'Some philosophers are lonely.' The notation wasn't the Polish one of course, for I had no time to consult my text-book, but the canonical one to which I was more accustomed; nor was the message particularly well chosen or incisive. I didn't think this would matter much, though: what was important was that the intent to communicate be recognisable.

Whiskers was gazing out of the window, her attention momentarily claimed by Sister Lucy and the gardener, who seemed to be having an argument over the lawn-mower – in point of fact Sister Lucy seemed to be aiming kicks at the machine and the gardener trying to dissuade her, so such rapt attention was understandable.

Had I been at all secretive, I think I might have betrayed the irregularity of what I was doing, but I acted instead quite openly and calmly, picked up the book, riffled through it, wrote my message and handed it back to her. Had it been premeditated, I should never have brought it off with such aplomb. As it was she noticed nothing.

I had by now become irreversibly excited about what I was doing, though blighting this excitement was a sneaking sense of not having acted quite fairly towards the Chaplain. However, I reflected, the next move was up to the inhabitant of the turret; if I received no encouragement from that quarter I would let the matter drop. If I did receive encouragement, then Hugh was quite simply in the wrong in protecting the isolation of a creature who wished instead for company. Either way therefore I was acting perfectly correctly. But notwithstanding the cogency of these reflections, I preferred not to dine with Jitters that evening, and bicycled off on my own for sandwiches and something a little stronger than beer.

All was quiet when I returned, and all the lights – both in the priest's cottage and in the main house – were off. As I wheeled my bike over the gravel, so interspersed with cut and growing grass that it made hardly any noise, I glanced up at the fatidical window. There was no flicker of light and no movement, but the turret dweller had by now become so real to me that I could almost sense his presence: he was lying awake in the darkness, maybe, listening to the minute sounds of my re-entry; or

44

else standing immobile at the window, watching. A sad case, Hugh had said, and I wondered what the sadness could possibly consist in if it were mitigated by incarceration. I parked my bicycle in the courtyard, where Jesus of the plaster heart stood bleeding. No. Isolation in a turret even if self-imposed was, I thought as I observed the solitary little statue, unlikely to render the case any less sad; and with a confirmed sense of having acted justly, I went off to bed.

The book – Mill's *System of Logic* – was returned the very next day, and, dissipating any residue of doubt that may still have been lurking in my subconscious, on the fly-leaf, directly below my own inscription, was pencilled clearly:

$$(x)\,(Px \rightarrow Lx)$$
$$Pm\ (U.E.)$$
$$/\therefore Lm$$

I stared incredulously at the message. The individual constant 'm' must surely stand for 'me' or 'myself', making the last line – the conclusion – read: 'Therefore I am lonely.' It touched me more deeply than if I had witnessed the philosopher in the flesh, struggling to regain his freedom. I think it must have been on account of the contrast between the bare logical form of the message and its poignant content. Here plainly was a human being denouncing with dignity and simplicity a miserable, perhaps even intolerable situation. This was no epistolary exchange between dilettante philosophers – it was a cry for help. What was I to do now, I wondered.

'Professor! Professor! Are you awake? Professor?'

I felt a stab of anguish as for a brief moment the youthfulness of the voice tricked me into placing it in the stream of my recollections, for anything as if I was still being called on across the intervening years for help – help that I had given then so gladly and so badly – and it took me several seconds to readjust to the present and to realise that there was someone at the door, calling my name. My hands were shaking, and it took me further seconds to grope for my glasses and get up to open the door. On the threshold stood a large, plump girl, wearing an ungainly modern compromise between plain-clothes and religious habit, a get-up which made her look not so much the contemporary nun which she presumably was as a kind of social misfit – a half-caste product of sacred and secular, dressed wrongly for either sphere. Two massive calves protruded from under the unfashionably long skirt like a couple of prickly pears.

'I'm so sorry, Professor,' she blurted out uncomfortably, enabling me to read off from her expression what a sight I must look, 'I didn't like to disturb you, only it's nearly suppertime and we were wondering whether you would like to come and join the others for a bite of something.' She shifted her considerable weight uneasily from one pear to the other. 'Or else I could bring you up some biscuits and a hot drink, if you would rather. I mean, it would be no trouble. You'll be needing all your strength for tomorrow.'

I would indeed, but it was disconcerting to hear her say so. I put my hand to my head to try and steady both, and opted as politely as I could for solitude and biscuits. Anamnesis was painful enough without the added burden of having to make interim conversation to a gathering of total strangers.

'Oh, I see. You're not here with the party then. Not

here for the big "do" tomorrow. How silly of me.' A reassured expression began to dawn on the worried, eager face and she gave a pleasingly spontaneous giggle. 'What an oaf I am! Well, I'll be right back with your tray. Do say if there is anything else you need. If you'd like a wash and brush-up, there's a bathroom and a you-know-what just along . . . '

'That's perfectly all right,' I managed to say. 'It's very kind of you, but I have all I need, thank you, and I already know my way around. I have been here before.'

'Oh, splendid, splendid!' said the nun, 'I'll be back in a jiffy,' and she made off at a springy run, leaving me there in the doorway, dishevelled and in my stockinged feet – one foot inside the turret and one out. I could hear laughter and voices from the other room near by; a group of young people were coming up the stairs carrying luggage, and an older couple walked past my door giving me a friendly nod as they passed.

Splendid, splendid that I had been here before, the kindly young nun had said. How wrong she was. It was anything but splendid; it was agony. My mental state, in fact, closely matched that of my body – the same tremulousness, the same dishevelment, and the same hybrid stance, with one foothold in the busy, matter-of-fact flux of the present, one in the lonely and petrified atmosphere of the past: a static, irrevocable, immutable past which yet possessed the paradoxical power to surprise and frighten.

I waited just where I was until my tray-bearer returned, unwilling to leave the comparative peace of this no-man's-land in time. Then I took my food in the manner of a fugitive animal and stepped back into the small, hexagonal room to wrestle once more with my memories. I had plenty of time. It was strange, but I

47

could tell now from the mere feel of the place that she was no longer there.

It hadn't felt like that when I had arrived – perhaps I had even, with some part of my mental equipment, been hoping or fearing to find her – or traces of her – still there, still reachable; but now I knew calmly and absolutely that she was dead and had been so for a long time. The knowledge came to me with no accompanying feelings: no pain, no regret, no surprise.

The drink was lukewarm but the biscuits crisp and good. Munching on one, I began to plod dutifully back to where I had left the thread of reminiscence and to pick it up again from there.

3

The most straightforward and natural exit from my quandary as to what I should do, now that I had confirmed not only the presence of the prisoner but also his reluctant solitude (yes, I had truly started thinking of him as a prisoner, although as yet with a certain dose of amused and voluntary exaggeration), was to go straight to the Abbess and ask her quite openly for an explanation. And this in fact was what I did. More or less, that is. I went to the Abbess, but I did not go straight to her, nor did I go openly; I chose instead a more cautious and winding route.

It had occurred to me to start with Jitters and to try and nail him down to responsibilities that, in view of his position as Chaplain, were partly his, but this would have entailed admitting to a certain amount of not exactly dishonesty but at least casuistry on my part; besides which, I had already received a fairly graphic impression of his likely behaviour in a critical situation. He would flap his feathery, neurotic hands at me and beg me blindly to desist. This in all conscience I could no longer do. No, it would be better and kinder to leave Jitters out of this.

How then about Sister Frogface? I recalled the sharp look she had given me when I had first noticed the turret

49

window; she was evidently conversant with the situation, but quite as evidently she would brook no interlopers. No, Frogface with her strong reserves of willpower would never do.

Finally, therefore, I decided that the only course of action open to me which did not involve, but at the same time did not prejudice, downright deceit – for in my heart of hearts this, I knew, was what I should eventually have to resort to – was somehow to sound out the Reverend Mother without her realising what I was about. The strategy I chose was thus not only indirect, but involved a certain amount of deviousness: deviousness which of course could always be revoked when and if I encountered in the Abbess a potential ally, or at least a reasonable fellow human being who was prepared, unlike the others so far, to speak frankly on this unhealthily secret question. She, of all people, would also have the authority to do so, should she so wish. So, having settled on my course, I decided to bluff a little and to use my own brand of authority – that of the physician. The resulting conversation – for which I had to make a formal request and post it in a kind of dummy letter-box outside the august lady's reception room – was cryptic all right, but turned out still less illuminating than I had hoped: I found myself confronting not so much ally or enemy, as a blank, rubbery and impenetrable wall.

Popeye's parlour was decorated unsubtly in the Madonna's own traditional colours. Her desk was covered by a speckless white lace cloth, and she sat behind it in a powdery blue penumbra, a pen in her hand unflanked by any other writing materials, her watery eyes scrutinising some unspecifiable fugue-point beyond the door which I had just opened.

'Ah Doctor, do please come in. So kind of you to find

the time for a little chat. I would have suggested it myself, only . . .' and she laid down the pen with a sigh as if it were weighing on her heavily. 'I hope you are finding everything to your satisfaction? For myself I am extremely satisfied with the way you are righting our precious library.' She had never been near the place to my knowledge. 'What is it exactly that you wanted to see me about?'

I inhaled deeply and went straight – although as I have already intimated that is an inappropriate adverb – about my business. 'I am here', I began a shade pompously, 'in my capacity as medical practitioner rather than that of librarian. I am sure you are attended by a competent local doctor . . . ' Here I paused for confirmation, but the bulbous eyes stared bleakly on, ' . . . and it is not at all my wish to interfere with his practice, but there are one or two little things I have noticed which I should like to call your attention to, so that you can then refer them to your GP if you think fit.'

'Very kind,' she replied flatly, but I noticed that, dissociating itself from the expressionless remainder, her left toe had begun to tap impatiently.

'I am a little worried about Sister Lobelia,' I said earnestly (this of course was Whiskers, the vicarious reader), a comment which seemed to generate in the Abbess symptoms of rapidly worsening deafness. I refrained from repeating it or expanding on it, however, until granted some kind of reaction, verbal or otherwise.

'Yes?' she queried after a long delay, her voice still cautiously flat.

'I think she is seriously overstraining her eyesight. She reads a great deal, you know,' I said with heavy emphasis and waited again. 'Very widely, too,' I added, trying to convey a different kind of concern.

This ruffled her. The toe tapped faster and she picked

up the pen and began rolling it between finger and thumb.

'I am well acquainted with Sister Lobelia's love of reading,' she said more sharply, gazing fixedly at the wall behind me, 'and our own doctor has already issued her with reading glasses. You need have no worries on that score. What else did you wish to see me about?' So that path led nowhere. Her curtness was plain enough, but it was impossible to tell whether it was an evasive curtness, or whether she was merely resenting my interference. Nor did one possibility exclude the other. Knowing I was in for another snub, but hoping it would prove more enlightening, I tried another tack: 'I am also concerned', I said, 'about the state of Father Hugh's health.'

The toe stopped tapping: she had a ready answer to that one. 'Father Hugh is a very sick man,' she explained meticulously, 'I'm sure you don't need me to tell you that, but your concern is understandable. It does you credit. You can rest assured though that every care is being taken. Every possible care. He is being treated by a very well-known London doctor – perhaps you will have heard of him, although he is of course much *older* than yourself,' and she mentioned proudly the impressive name.

Snub number two. I nodded gravely and resumed, 'It is not so much his physical state I was alluding to. I am sure he is in the very best of hands. No, it is – how shall I put it – rather his psychological condition.'

Tap, tap, tap, very fast this time: impatience was turning into annoyance. 'Psychology, psychiatry, philosophy or whatever,' she rapped out quite tartly – although the confusion of terms was I think genuine and not intended as part of her disparagement – 'we have little use for that kind of thing here. I think I am right,

Doctor, in assuming that you yourself are not a religious man?' I gave her a tender smile, but no reply.

'Well, be that as it may,' she said, blotting her eyes with an incongruously grimy handkerchief, her lids seeming to have no restraining function whatever, 'here, you must realise, our concern is not with the psyche, as you call it, but with the soul. Take care of the soul and the psyche will take care of itself. And there is really very little to worry about in the case of Father's soul. He is a very holy man, you know. A very holy man.' Her gaze now came to rest on the ceiling, as if finding grounds there for this statement.

'I think he is a very lonely man,' I said bluntly, 'and loneliness or worse still, enforced solitude . . . ' Here I paused, to let what I hoped was the lateral significance of my words sink in, although I felt bound to admit that the allusions which had seemed so cunning when I had thought them up were sadly inadequate: so far I had extracted nothing more explicit than a little foot tapping and pen rolling – quite normal reactions when your hired librarian comes blundering in during his working hours to sneak on a myopic nun and to hint that your Chaplain is not quite right in the head. '. . . enforced solitude', I repeated with obdurate stress, 'is a bad thing for anyone.'

The Abbess sniffed impatiently, giving no sign of latching on to my double entendre. Perhaps, however, the last gauche remark about Father Hugh had scored: it should have made her righteously indignant; instead she bent low over the lacy cloth and asked circumspectly, 'Has Father spoken to you of anything in particular, that you should come to me about this? Has he told you, I mean, that he feels . . . how shall I put it . . . ? Not entirely happy with us? Not fully at his ease?'

Here at last was perhaps the shadow of an indication.

Could it not be that Popeye was worried lest the Chaplain, in a weak moment after a third or fourth beer, had told me something he shouldn't have? I watched her closely but there was no telling: the veiled head remained bent, the body still. Realising that I would get no further information from this quarter, I decided that it was safer to backtrack now than to risk raising further suspicions. No, no, I hastened to reassure her, Father Hugh had never so much as intimated to me dissatisfaction over any aspect of his life or work at the Convent; I had merely myself interpreted . . . and on I went in my chosen role of over-zealous well-wisher, trotting out a string of commonplaces about the subconscious and its wily ways of finding somatic expression.

The Abbess, under the opinion, I think, that I was airing the views of a friend of mine by the name of Fred, gave me a few minutes of incredulous attention before cutting me short. 'I am grateful for what you have told me, Doctor,' she said stonily, all circumspection reabsorbed once more into explicit impatience, 'and for sparing me some of your valuable time. Your opinion is that Father Hugh is in a – what did you call it? – a delicate psychological state. My own is that his bodily state is delicate, while his spiritual state is one of deep and enviable serenity. His mind, if that is what you are perhaps talking about, does not to my way of thinking need medical attention. It is, as I said, our policy to leave things like that in the hands of the Lord: He never sends us more trials than we can bear, you know. If He sees fit to send us suffering,' here she performed a further energetic mopping of the leaky lids, 'it is because He has already provided us with the requisite fortitude.'

I murmured authentic surprise.

'We shall all pray hard for Father, I can assure you. That is *our* kind of psycho-what-have-you; the only one we place our faith in. You too will be in our prayers, Doctor.' With this she dropped the pen neatly on the table and rose to her feet: the interview was over.

Its results could hardly be termed positive, except for the fact that I now felt free to go ahead with my plans undisturbed by scruples. Wherever I had turned I had so far encountered nothing but concealment and evasiveness. With this last probe, although it had not served any concrete purpose beyond that of showing me up as a conceited meddler, and of sealing for ever the already slender channels of communication between the Abbess and myself, the course of action open to me was clearer than ever. Although I had failed to identify conclusively either the leader or the participants in the conspiracy of secrecy against the poor turret philosopher, I felt that my visit to the Abbess had as it were given them, whoever 'they' might turn out to be, a formal choice of strategy: a sort of covert ultimatum in choice of weapons. They, not I, had opted for deceit. Yes, I could now go ahead with my plans.

Not that I had really organised my ideas to the point of being able to describe them as a plan. I had one firm intention and that was to make personal contact with the hidden individual – the 'prisoner' of my private reference, still thought of in inverted commas, although increasingly faint ones – who had sent me the chilling, logical *cri de coeur*. The obvious time to choose was that very night, for both speed and secrecy were called for, but beyond that I had very little idea of what my intervention was to consist in: I would go to the turret, I decided, and then I would see. I was thus quite unprepared for what I in fact did see, but then no amount of preparation would have quite cushioned me against that.

I had supper as usual with my jumpy friend. I mentioned nothing to him about my morning talk with our mutual employer, nor did I question him further over the refugee, and maybe this very omission made him suspect that I might be up to something, for he led the conversation laboriously to the topic of scientific inquiry and from there to curiosity *tout court*, making it quite difficult for me to keep the discussion at our habitually elegant level of abstraction. Amongst other things, I remember him musing at one point as to how and why curiosity should be said to have proved disastrous to the proverbial cat. 'Do you think it is a corruption of some name or other, Wig?' he suggested, giving me a funny, arch little smile. 'Curiosity killed Richardt? Or killed Taggart? More likely a German than a Scot, don't you think – nosing about in things that didn't concern him and meeting a sticky end?'

'Hmm,' I grunted, deploring his taste in tactics and trying to think up a suitably tasteless answer. 'More likely to have been a Catherine or a Kate, though; only the moral drawn was the wrong one. Curiosity never killed anything other than ignorance. Like when people talk of "idle" curiosity. Curiosity is never idle; it's the busiest thing there is.' Warming to the subject, I added in a louder and sterner register, 'Curiosity, believe me, Hugh, makes the world go round. Or rather it makes us aware that it is going round; and that in turn is a step towards making it go round the way we want it to. We certainly wouldn't be sitting here drinking beer if somebody hadn't wondered what brewed hops tasted like, would we? And again, just out of curiosity, how is our supply going?' I had insisted we set up a joint fund for beer and tobacco; it had seemed only correct at the start, but from a medical point of view it was proving badly mistaken, for with the reduction of the financial burden

Hugh was now drinking and smoking almost double his former intake.

The mention of beer did the trick. He pottered off willingly, and I was able to use his absence to make a quick sortie to the front of the house: light was filtering out of the turret window, and a pile of sheets and blankets hung there limply in the damp night air. It looked as if someone was taking advantage of the late hour to give the room an airing. A nun's silhouette appeared, gave the bedclothes a feeble shaking and yanked them in again. I stepped back stealthily among the trees, rounded the corner and walked slowly back to the presbytery to find Jitters returning with the beer. Mercifully he had set the topic of curiosity aside.

'Better put your thinking-cap on, Wig. It's free will and determinism for us tonight!' he announced gleefully as he settled the tray and began pouring; so it was on this time-hollowed issue that we set to that evening.

We talked, the pair of us, late on into the night, going through all the familiar and comfortable stages of skirmish, until, feigning a sleepiness that I was far from feeling, I took my leave. As always, Hugh was reluctant to see me go – I fear that his illness procured him amongst other drawbacks chronic insomnia – and it took me the best part of twenty minutes to make a clean getaway. When I did, it was to leave him there, still sitting outside among the ghostly, nodding roses, the white blur of his face distinguishable from theirs only in size. I hoped he would not sit there all night: the presbytery was well out of earshot, but none the less I needed to feel myself completely alone for my undertaking. Back in my turret I waited therefore for what must have been another full hour before setting out, filling in the time by reading and by paring all twenty of my nails. I washed too and changed. Quite why, I do not know, unless I unconsciously felt the extreme importance of the coming visit and the need to underline this in a concrete, corporeal way. I was not at all nervous – just pleasantly excited – and as untroubled now by qualms as a boy-scout resolving on his good deed for the day.

It was close on two a.m. when I finally ventured out into the corridor, but a last glimpse of my window told me that the occupant of the counterpart turret was still – and quite literally – burning the midnight oil, for there came a steady, weak glow from the window across the way.

Listening very attentively, I edged my way down the long passage. The light from a very round but already waning moon illuminated the flagstones in the courtyard, where the sorry little Christ stood hedged in by prickly cacti. He too looked as if he needed rescuing.

I reached the antechamber to the turret without any incident. All was quiet. On my side this antechamber was more of an extended corridor than a room; it had no door, merely a kind of arch, its only function being to give access to the turret itself. Here instead there was a door, firmly closed.

I stood in front of it a few moments and then put my eye to the keyhole: darkness. There was a funny smell, though. I put one nostril to the keyhole and sniffed deeply. Soap. It must be a bathroom; perhaps the prisoner's private bathroom. If so it was presumably locked. I tried the handle gingerly and contrary to my expectations the door opened easily. It was a bathroom all right, for my groping hands made contact with the hard rim of a basin, and, groping further, with its content of water, in which floated an amorphous, stringy mass, like seaweed. Since the door to the turret could only lie straight ahead, I pushed cautiously on, inches at a time, through the sweet-smelling darkness, holding my dripping hands before me as buffers. The floor was slippery, and my foot had become entangled in some kind of cloth or garment: I bent down and disentangled it with difficulty, and as I did so my breath squeezed out as from a bellows, making me realise that I had been holding it far too long. By the time I reached the opposite door my previous state of expectant calm had degenerated into one of anxiety, uncomfortably close to fright. For who, I wondered, was there on the other side of the door? And what if after all they had no wish to see me? What if they were actually to resent my chosen form of overture? They might even take fright themselves and cry out, and I should then be found by the nuns, snooping about in this undignified, underhand way with no better justification than a terse little scribbling of symbolic logic which anybody might have written. I reflected hastily that it would perhaps be more prudent to go back to my own room and to spend the next few days in making sure that the prisoner (who might anyway be no prisoner at all but a bedridden invalid or even a dangerous lunatic – you can see how rattled I was getting at this point) really wanted to see me. Having come so far, though, I thought it would be a shame not to investigate just a little further, so I put my eye to the second keyhole and squinted into the room.

A candle was burning low on a saucer, and by its wavering light I could make out a slight, seated figure, hunched over a book. This was nothing more nor less than I had expected: the unexpected thing, and which made me experience a wave of almost physical sickness so distressing did it seem, was that the reader, although apparently dressed in a perfectly ordinary way other-wise, had his head enveloped in a cloth bag. Not only that, but with one hand he seemed to be pressing the bag against his face in order to facilitate his reading.

I drew back from the keyhole, profoundly shocked,

and started backing rapidly away from the door. My foot got caught again, and as I stood there balancing on one leg and frantically trying to free myself from what seemed now to be inexplicably a piece of female under-wear, a thin, worried voice called out softly, 'Who's there?' and then more worriedly still, 'Is anyone there?' So my prisoner was female. This fact, together with the anxiety in the voice and the mundaneness of the garment I was holding in my hand, served to calm me instantly. I went back to the door and whispered clearly,

'It's me, the librarian. I got your message.'

There was a gasp, and the small, hooded figure came rapidly towards the door, obscuring my field of vision.

'Ah,' came the voice, 'I can't let you in, you know.'

So much the better, I thought to myself, still greatly perturbed by the eerie headgear.

'But we can talk', it went on, 'only quietly. We mustn't be found out. Who are you?'

'I told you: the librarian.'

'Yes, I know. But I mean what's your name? Where do you come from besides the library? You don't sound English and you don't sound old, and you don't sound at *all* as if you were a nun.'

I gave her all the information she asked for, although there was scarcely room to fit it in between the peppering of questions which she went on asking with mounting excitement: Was I here for long? Where had I studied logic? Had she got the symbols right? Had I studied Kant? Could I help her with the pure unity of appercep-tion? Could I obtain barley sugar for her if she gave me the coupons? Did I sleep in the other turret, because she was sure somebody did? Then she halted abruptly, struck by one of my answers. 'What did you say? A doctor? You've been sent to see me then?' she said slowly, her voice suddenly stiff and mistrustful.

I tried to explain the quiescent nature of my true profession, but could not have sounded very convincing, as the fountain of questions trickled to a halt, to be replaced by a wary breathing, muffled by the bag; then she cleared her throat and said drily and finally, 'Goodnight, then, Doctor – what's your name? – Ludwig. Herr Doktor, gute Nacht,' and began to move away from the door.

'Wait a minute,' I whispered urgently. 'I only came to see you because of your message. Only because of that. No one sent me. I won't come back again if you don't want me to, I promise. Only please tell me,' the words were coming out in a rush now, as it seemed direly important to hold her attention and thus prevent her definitive withdrawal, 'even if you don't want me to come back – especially, rather, if you don't want me to come back because otherwise I shall come back and back until you do – you aren't being held here against your will, are you? I must know this. It is what I came to find out. Are you locked in? Do the nuns allow you out if you want? *Do* you ever go out? And . . .'

Here I hesitated. I badly wanted to know about the head-bag, but didn't know how to set about asking.

'Yes?' She sounded less wary now and had moved no further off.

'You haven't told me what your name is,' I said.

'Martina. That's what the "m" was for: Martina.'

'I see. Martina,' I said, trying out this name – a name which unbeknownst to me was shortly to take on such varied and ineradicable connotations – for the first time, and using it just this once as a mere device to call her by, 'Martina, what exactly is that thing you are wearing on your head?'

Silence. Then the faint, muffled voice said, 'So you *do* know.'

61

'Know what?' I asked cautiously.

'That there is something wrong with me.'

'No, Martina,' I replied gently. 'I know nothing about you at all, I assure you. I have been taken on to sort out the books in the library. That's how I found out about you – by noticing the books. No one has told me anything, if that's what's worrying you. No one except Father Hugh, that is, and he only told me that you existed; that you were a refugee. I thought you must be a man – an old man. Really. I thought you were just an old man in a tower.'

She made a brief grunting noise which I classified as a laugh and then said thoughtfully, 'Father Hugh is the nicest person here.'

'I think so too,' I agreed readily. 'He is my only friend here. We have supper together every evening. How about coming out of your turret and having supper with us one evening in Father Hugh's house? Wouldn't you like that, Martina? Do you think it could be arranged?'

There was a long pause, then I heard her moving about inside and a needle of brighter light shone through the keyhole; she had turned the electric light on.

'That would be nice,' she replied politely. Then, 'I don't go out much as a rule, you know, but there is no need for you to worry. It is my own choice. I like it here. I have everything I want. As a matter of fact I did go out today, though. I went out to pick some flowers – they are right there in the wash basin: so you see I really can come and go as I like.'

'Ah,' I said, happier about the seaweed but not entirely convinced. 'Show me the key then. Just show it to me,' I added hurriedly, as I still didn't want her to go unlocking the door until I had found out about the reason for the strange head-gear.

'The key?'

'Yes, the key to the door; so that I know you aren't locked in.'

'Oh, but I'm not – only, the key . . . ' There were rummaging sounds, then a pleased 'Ah, here it is!'

'Hold it up to the keyhole,' I said, 'where I can see it.'

'So *that's* what you've been doing,' she stated with a trace of scorn. 'Looking through the keyhole. I don't think that was a very nice thing to do,' and she held up a small ornamental key for my inspection, much too delicate for the lock.

'Fine!' I said tactfully. 'So you can get out if you want to. That's fine then. Don't worry, I'm not going to ask you to let me in; I just wanted to be sure. You haven't told me about that thing on your head, though. I am a *sort* of doctor, you know, so I could well understand if . . . ' Here tact began to fail me, however, for what on earth could you ask a person so grievously afflicted as to shroud their face and hide themselves away in a tower? 'If you are disfigured?' 'If you are deformed?' No, much too blunt.

' . . . Was it something that happened to you during the war?' I proceeded tentatively.

This time the silence was a very long one.

'There's no need for you to tell me,' I began again, using as quiet and matter-of-fact a tone as I could devise, 'only it would be hard for you to surprise me.' (Hard, but as things turned out not impossible.) 'I'm used to all sorts of . . . ' My voice slowed as I tried to find another circumlocution, but she interrupted me. 'My cover? It's velvet. It's really very soft. Quite comfortable when you are used to it. You are a great worrier, Dr Ludwig. And I don't wear it often. What day is it?'

I recalled the menu without effort. 'Thursday. Why? What has that to do with it?'

'I mean what date?'

I was not so sure of this. 'I think it must be the twenty-fourth,' I ventured.

'Ah. Well then if you come back tomorrow, or better still let's say the day after, I won't be wearing it any more. You will come back, won't you? Ludwig?'

I had been doing some rapid thinking. 'Yes,' I said, 'I'll be back tomorrow. Only not tomorrow night. Tomorrow daytime.' My thinking had brought me to the conclusion that the more varieties of light that were let in on this business the better. 'I am going to speak to the Abbess first thing in the morning, and then I am coming up here to see you and to take you out for another walk.'

There came a long, wan sigh from the other side of the door. 'Don't do that, Ludwig. Just come back. Like you did tonight.' This checked me. Did she think it possible I would be refused permission, I wondered. Was there indeed a likelihood of this happening? I gave a reassuring laugh. 'Liebes Kind!' I said. I don't know quite how, but I had correctly decided that she must be very young. 'Liebes Kind, you don't seriously think that a crowd of thick-headed old spinsters will prevent me from seeing you, do you? I am simply going to announce that I want to: that we both want to. The whole thing is to be quite open from now on. They'll have a job to try and stop me. Why, I'll call in the police if necessary and tell them you're being held prisoner.'

'But I'm not,' she commented in a shocked whisper.

'No, of course you're not,' I said, 'but that's what I'll tell them.'

'Well, I don't know,' she said, giving another funny, blanketed laugh, 'if you really think it is better for us to meet in the daytime . . .'

'I really do think that,' I put in firmly. 'We can't have much of a conversation if we always have to whisper through a keyhole, can we? I was hoping you might like to discuss philosophy with me – there could hardly be a more uncomfortable place for it than this.'

'Then I think you should ask Sister Lucy about it,' she said slowly, 'not the Reverend Mother. If you ask her correctly I think she will say yes.'

'And what do you think "correctly" would be?' I asked.

'I don't know, Ludwig. That must be up to you to find out.'

And so it was that the next morning found me, instead of attending to my duties as librarian, prowling around assiduously in the tracks of Sister Lucy like an unsure suitor, trying to catch her in one of her rare moments of inoperative solitude.

The conversation of the previous night had ended a little vexingly. I was certain now that this Martina creature wanted to go on seeing me, and I was equally sure that, although technically not a prisoner, her liberties were being – though perhaps for some valid reason – seriously curtailed. What I was not so sure of was whether I wanted to go on seeing her. The shrouded head had been extremely disturbing: the more so since she had studiously avoided answering my question about it. It bespoke either physical or psychical infirmity of a particularly grave nature, and either way the tenor of our proposed philosophical discussions would be marred. Whiskers might have been preferable after all, I thought regretfully, for what is a millimetre or two of facial hair compared to outright lunacy or a disfigurement so unsightly that the bearer has to conceal it even from herself when alone and in a darkened room? Perhaps, though, it was some blemish of traumatic origin, and was on the mend. Anyway, whatever it was I should soon know, and it could hardly prove more alarming than having to converse with a velvet bag.

On the positive side there was however, I reflected, the promise of the voice, which had sounded so young and so vivacious.

Frogface was certainly having a busy morning. I was obliged to alter my opinions on the consolations of contemplative life as I watched her bustling progress: skirts hitched up like a huntress, she strode purposefully from place to place, giving advice closely resembling orders to the gardener, supervising the worker Sisters, acting as a liaison officer between the Abbess's still parlour and the busy kitchen regions of the Bursar. Every so often she would repair for a few minutes to her own headquarters, situated in a poky little cupboard-cum-hidey-hole under the main staircase, where I hesitated to beard her on account of a large 'Do not disturb' notice hanging on the doorhandle, fiercely underscored in black and red ink. I was on the point of giving up and returning belatedly to my own work when I spotted her, breviary in hand, setting off towards the cemetery at a more sober pace, her skirts restored to ground level. When I called after her, instead of showing irritation at being deprived of her well-deserved pause for meditation, her face lit up enthusiastically. 'Well, well! Ludwig our librarian. I may call you Ludwig, mayn't I? If it hadn't been for my vocation I suppose I could well have a son your age by now. Now that's a funny thought!' and thus saying she latched herself firmly on to my arm and began steering me at a strong rhythmic pace towards the graveyard, chattering animatedly and granting me a few calculated insights into her personal history as we went, so far as I could make out with the principal object of obliquely conveying to a fresh listener the splendours of her past existence.

'My favourite place for a little quiet reading,' she sighed contentedly, coming to the end of her brief life-history at the very spot where it was likely to find one day its physical completion also, 'no one else but me seems to come here, and I do sometimes, I must admit, feel the need to be alone. Alone, or,' she added in courteous aftersight, 'with someone I can really have a good talk to, like yourself, Ludwig. You know what I mean?' I did indeed. She meant that the rest of the community boasted nothing but cultural and social inferiors. I gave a tenth or eleventh understanding murmur.

'My life is a full one though, you know,' she added, tucking the breviary inside her sleeve and throwing back her head in relaxed enjoyment of the sunshine and the graves.

'But you do know!' she said briskly in a changed tone, fishing about for her pink spectacles, and placing them firmly on her nose. 'You do know, of course. You've been following me around all morning. There's not much I don't notice. Surely not for the sake of "*mes beaux yeux*"?' and she fluttered her pale lashes behind the goggles in mock flirtation. Well, perhaps not so very mock, either.

'I wanted to talk to you,' I said candidly, for there was nothing to be gained by hedging when the pink lenses were trained on their target. 'I wanted to talk to you about Martina.'

'Ah!' said Frogface, showing no surprise but continuing to watch me with intense concentration. 'So you've rooted her out, eh, our solitary Miss? I knew that was bound to happen. Now I suppose you want to see her – or have you seen her already?' Trying to withstand the refractory glare of her scrutiny, I told her more or less the full story of my investigations to date, soft-pedalling the curiosity and stressing instead the frankly humanitarian reasons which had prompted me to carry them out and to employ such roundabout tactics.

'Yes, yes,' she commented unperturbed, 'I suppose it would seem like that from the outside. The thing is . . .' and she took my wrist in a friendly grasp, giving it an appreciative squeeze with the tips of her fingers, ' . . . Nice hands you've got. Nice nails. The thing is, that Martina is inclined to be a little over-dramatic about her plight. Not of course that it is exactly a rosy one. She came to us when she was quite a child; farmed out on us by a refugee organisation during the war. They didn't seem to know what to do with her. She had been in some kind of institution for orphaned children to begin with, and then she had been sent to a couple of families, but she hadn't been able to settle down anywhere. Couldn't – or wouldn't – fit in. Poor child. She was in a bad state when she arrived. No relatives, of course; no possessions; precious little of anything, really, memories included. Just a medical report, which is probably still lying around somewhere. I could dig it out for you if you are interested.' She paused for a moment in the transparent hope of gauging the extent of my curiosity, but I merely nodded dutifully and asked her to continue.

'Well,' she said, 'the war was still on, and what with one thing and another . . . we were turned into an eye hospital during the war, you know. You didn't? Well we were . . . no one had much time for the poor little thing. She was left very much to her own devices. Come to think of it, that may not have been such a bad thing after all, because she began to spend more and more time over her reading. She's a regular bookworm now. No interest in religion though: I suppose you've noticed that, and,' unfurling a knowing grin, 'I don't suppose it worries you much either.' Then she added in confidential aside as if furnishing an explanation: 'The family was originally Jewish, I believe.'

We had been walking in and out of the graves in a

sedate slalom; now Sister Lucy bunched up her skirts and sat firmly down on one of the mounds. 'All friends here,' she said, patting the grass beside her, 'no one to mind. Sit yourself down.'

I hitched up my trouser legs dubiously before sitting down and glanced at the grey stone cross which acted as sole garnish to the grave: it was, I noticed with surprise, devoid of all inscription. I looked round more heedfully: there were in fact no inscriptions anywhere – the graves were all uniformly blank. All, that is, except for one in the very furthest corner which was marked by a dull red marble headstone in place of the usual cross, and which bore a short lettered inscription, too small and distant to be legible.

Frogface must have been watching me closely still, for she said, quite unprompted, 'No, that's right. No names for us here any more. We hardly ever use our names after entering the Order, and we certainly don't need them when we die. No point in commemorating an old suit of clothes that has been discarded, is there?'

My eyes rested for a moment on her full, capable body, terminating in its pair of congruously stout shoes, sitting easily atop the buried remains of one of her companions and smiling in the sunlight, and felt something close to admiration. Not only dying but also living must, I reckoned enviously, be made smoother by possessing such a remarkably insouciant attitude towards mortality. As if sensing my admiration, Frogface adjusted her habit complacently across the wide-planted knees and resumed where she had left off in her account.

'Well, as I was saying, Martina just went her own way. At first there was the language barrier too, so we didn't really worry about schooling. Just left her alone. Sometimes I do rather feel that we should have done a little more,' she blinked at me appealingly, 'but as I said there was the war, and the hospital, and then she seemed really happier on her own. Yes, it was probably not such a bad thing.'

This reiteration was presumably intended as a prompter for my approbation, but I said nothing. There were too few elements for me to form a judgment on, and the one that I had none the less formed was not lenient towards the nuns. Besides, I was still worrying about the head-bag. Had she come here with it on, I wondered? And the tragic image of a small, enshrouded waif flashed before my mind's eye, standing before the huge grey portals, begging admittance to a house full of busy strangers with no time for her and no will to understand.

'Yes, it may well have been all for the best,' Frogface went on breezily, all misgivings autonomously resolved. 'She picked up English in no time at all – she is a very bright little thing, you know; oh yes, *very* bright – and the better her English got, the more she read and the more time she spent in the turret. And then she began locking herself in. No, wait. There was a time when she became friendly with one of the patients – a young airman – and I think it was not until after he went and died that she started actually locking herself in . . . ' Her gaze strayed to the marble headstone as she said this, and then darted rapidly back to me, granting me for a brief instant the insight that she was sifting pieces of information in her mind and letting only a small quantity of them emerge.

'Why is she wearing that mask?' I asked baldly in order to hinder the sifting. 'Is she deformed or something?'

Frogface gave a start of surprise. 'Good Lord, no!' she said roundly. 'No, no, no, no, no, nothing of the kind. That's just another of her fads. Another way of being dramatic. That and the seclusion. She can come out whenever she wishes: you do realise that? No, there's nothing like that wrong with her. In fact, apart from the shyness there is very little wrong with her at all. Certainly nothing physical, that is. It might do her the world of good to have someone new to chat to.' She looked at me with a dubiousness in contrast to her tone. 'Yes, yes; then that's settled. You're sure she wants to see you, though, and not the other way round?'

'Both ways round,' I confirmed. 'We have a mutual interest in philosophy.'

'Oh yes, of course – philosophy.' She blew a jet of air from mouth to nostrils. 'She's a great one on the philosophy, is Martina. She would have done better to take up religion, though. I don't suppose she will ever leave us now, and it would have been a help to her if she had been able to share our life. Still, you never know. We always say a prayer for her conversion. You never know . . . '

She gave a cheerful sigh and rose sturdily to her feet: 'I think that *yes,*' she said, 'all things considered, it would be a good idea for you to see her.'

'The decision is ultimately yours?' I queried.

'Now, now, Ludwig,' and I got a severe prod on the breastbone, 'let's not put it that way, shall we? Let's say that Martina trusts my judgment. In me she has a friend, and not such a stupid one either. I think she realises that. The decision is yours, Ludwig, and Martina's too, of course. If you do decide to see her, though, keep in touch with me.'

'Keep in touch, I mean, at all times,' she added with a penetrating look, spacing out the last three words.

With the possible exception of that last utterance, my conversation with Frogface helped to restore to the curious atmosphere in which I had been living – atmosphere marked outwardly by nothing but long stretches of silence and time-arresting regularity, while conserving

71

inwardly the dense, impenetrable quality of a briar labyrinth – a sense of normality. I went about my afternoon work and study with equanimity once more. It had been settled that I was to meet Martina on the following afternoon. Sister Lucy had even suggested we borrow a second bicycle and go for a short trip round the neighbourhood. So it did begin to seem after all that my fears and suspicions had been groundless (otiose fruit of nothing but my own boredom and dissatisfaction) and that I had wilfully constructed the whole gothic edifice of melodrama – the wretched prisoner in the turret, the curtain of secrecy, the velvet mask veiling some horrible deformity, the guilty conspiracy of the nuns – in order to enliven my penurious and drab summer vacation. As I was tidying myself up before going over to supper at the presbytery, I leant out of the window and whistled across to the other turret and got a healthy, vigorous wave back from its inmate, who had, I could just perceive from that distance, doffed the bag in favour of what seemed to be a generous quantity of perfectly ordinary hair. I couldn't quite make out the colour, though, in the fading light, and this bothered me; I felt that the ingredient of colour would have added something a little more substantial to the picture.

I pulled on a sweater, piled up my books and left my room feeling relaxed and contented. I was looking forward to the evening meal and chat – hungry for both, in fact – and to telling my clerical friend the news of my suave success with Frogface over the matter of the recluse refugee. I reckoned that he too would be pleased at the air of normality which things were assuming, as long as I remembered to make it quite clear to him that I had in no way made use of the information he had given me, but had acted in parallel independence. As I walked over the grass, harrowed like a bas-relief by the long, trailing

72

shadows of the trees, I could hear what sounded like an argument going on: Jitters's voice was raised to an excited squeak and was producing a string of 'Dear, dear's' and 'No, no's'; but when I reached the cottage he came out to meet me alone and made no mention of whoever he had been talking to. They must have left by the rear entrance. The excitement however had remained with him, and although he made a pretence of slipping into our customary evening routine – dragging out the deckchairs, plumping himself down into one with a preparatory grunt, and fishing out from his cassock a much creased crossword which he had cut from the Convent's Sunday newspaper and on which he had been engaged for the best part of that week – I could see that he was in one of his edgiest moods. He waited however until the trolley had accomplished its crossing before unburdening himself to me. There was no question of informing him about my successful undertaking: he knew all about it already, and it constituted in effect the main part of his burden.

'What have you been up to, Wig?' he began plaintively as he helped himself to a slice of ropey, grey meat and similarly textured beans. 'What have you gone and done now, for the Lord's sake? I thought I told you not to meddle. What I told you, I told you in the strictest confidence – about the refugee, I mean. Now it seems you have betrayed this confidence . . . ' (Ha, ha, I thought, so the visitor was Frogface, and not a very truthful Frogface at that.)

He pushed his meat aside and laid down knife and fork with a clatter. 'What have you gone and done? I told you not to. I told you,' he repeated, looking at me reproachfully as if I were the sole cause of his inappetence.

Refusing to be infected by his nervousness, and clinging instead to the sense of matter-of-fact ordinariness that the morning's conversation with Frogface had infused into me, I explained as intended that my investigations had been entirely independent; that I had made virtually no use of the scarce information he had given me, that I had made no explicit promises to him, and that anyway even if I had I would still have considered that the need to investigate carried a more pressing moral claim.

'Nonsense, Wig!' he snapped tetchily. 'Sanctimonious claptrap! You and your curiosity. Virtue indeed! You're just after her because she's a girl, or because you're so anti-clerical that you think the nuns are bound to be up to shady tricks of some sort. Well, they're not, I can tell you.'

'I didn't know she was a girl,' I put in defensively – the other accusation was unanswerably correct. 'How old is she, anyway?'

'Under age,' said Jitters gloomily, with a tinge of satisfaction in his voice. 'I suppose you are all set to see her. Then go ahead. Go right ahead. All I can say is, look out.' He drew a circle in his gravy and stared at it; then he added quietly, so quietly that for a second I thought I must have heard amiss: 'Martina brings bad luck.'

This surprised me to the point of remonstrance, but he held up his hands in a warding-off gesture and said rapidly, 'No, Wig. Sorry. Don't mind me. I shouldn't have said that: it was wrong of me. A priest should never say a thing like that. But there is something about her – something . . . ' He snapped his fingers fast and feebly a dozen or so times, searching without success for a congruous, priestly way of expressing whatever it was that was preying on his mind, and then shrugged. 'Oh, leave it be. Something wrong, anyway,' he muttered. 'I did my best to keep you out of this business, but it's too late now. Go ahead. Have it your own way,' and with a dejected nod he went back to inspection of his meal. I questioned him further, of course, but all I could get out of him to back his whimsical opinion of the bad luck which Martina was alleged to bring was more or less what Sister Lucy had already told me concerning her past history: she had been shunted from institution to institution, from family to family, owing to a generic incapacity to 'fit in'; she had had a close childhood friend or cousin who had shared this fate until he had – perhaps in this luckier than she – found permanent accommodation by being killed in a banal domestic accident; she had had a second friend – the hospital patient – who had also died an early death: the bad luck seemed to me to be entirely and massively on her side.

This I told Jitters very firmly, and this time instead of arguing he agreed with me readily. Agreement even seemed to cheer him up, and from there our discussion began to take on a more relaxed and customary shape and to gravitate towards our usual oxymorous small-talk on large topics. We made quite a rowdy night of it in the end. I remember at one point being quite merciless in my attack against the popular, acritical 'It's not true of course, but I can't help believing it' attitude from which Hugh himself was anything but immune, and I remember too how he let my words – at times so fervent as to seem abusive – wash over and batter against him with evident pleasure, making not the least objection but appearing to bob happily like a cork on the strong wave of my certainty. I was on home ground here, of course, in what was in due time to become my own recognised province: science versus superstition; reasoned inquiry, method and proof versus fallacy, hearsay and ungrounded opinion. Small wonder that I managed to be so eloquent, so impassioned. Small wonder that Hugh, after we had got through the sixth bottle, began to wilt a little, and, after repeated enactments of watch-consulting, yawning and rhythmical tapping on the arms of the chair, to edge me gently towards the door. We bid each other a really friendly good-night, that night, and parted in the best of moods; I for once reluctant, though not too reluctant, to take my leave; Jitters pleased, but not too pleased, to see me go. But when I found myself trudging back to bed, still prey to the beer fumes and self-generated enthusiasm, I realised I had forgotten to ask about Martina's physical appearance – a subject that despite Frogface's reassurances still caused me a certain amount of trepidation, so I retraced my steps and poked my head through the lattice window of the sitting-room. Hugh was dusting ashtrays into the grate. He started violently as I called, and when he looked up I could see that his earlier agitation had already returned in full force.

'Oh, it's you again, Wig,' he said with a note of relief in his voice. 'What are you doing creeping about like that? You gave me quite a scare. Have you forgotten something?'

'Yes,' I said, 'I forgot to ask you. This Martina – what does she look like?'

'Look like? Oh, I see. What does she look like? Well . . . ' he said dully, giving an impatient twitch of the ashy handkerchief, 'little slip of a thing, really. Not much to look at. I'd be off to bed if I were you, Wig. You'll be seeing her tomorrow anyway.'

'Sorry, I just wanted to know,' I murmured apologetically. 'And her hair?'

'Hair? Just ordinary hair. Plenty of it.'

'I mean, what colour?'

'Red,' he replied, with a tired shiver. 'Very, very red. 'Night now, if that's all you wanted to know.'

I worked diligently all next morning. The thought of seeing the poor little Polish recluse made me strangely elated, and I was ashamedly aware that in some childish, illogical region of my brain, I had transformed the negative information that she was not deformed into an eager anticipation of her proving to be beautiful. I even found it hard to swallow down my lunch, and in the end was forced to wrap some of it up in a brown paper bag and store it for later – I could not risk sending it back untouched for fear the nuns diminish their already economical portions. Then, with an empty-feeling stomach and head, I made my way to the visitors' parlour where our first face-to-face meeting was to take place: no intervening head-bag this time, or at least so I sincerely hoped.

The girl, Martina, was already there, sitting composedly on one of the brittle upright chairs which flourished like flimsy mushrooms in all the Convent's reception rooms.

For someone who was to play such a major role in the admittedly slender cast of female characters in my life, and for someone who had been awarded by circumstances and by my own fertile imagination such an ornate build-up, she made an unincisive first impression. I should like to claim that I was immediately struck by her, or that I was at least penetrating enough to sense that I was in the presence of a human being of peculiar quality, but this was not so. I noticed, of course, the terrific blaze of her hair – so intense and vivid as to produce the unwelcome effect of obscuring the features it surrounded; but at the same time I could not help noticing the chunky and inelegant way in which it had been cut, and the equally clumsy cut of her clothes: a bundly flannel shirt tucked into a thick, pleated woollen skirt, and a pair of worn Franciscan sandals, not in any way enlivened by rolled-down beige stockings. Her face seemed nothing more than a white nucleus in a fiery setting, as flat and featureless on first inspection as an inverted fried egg; but here, as elsewhere in the long corollary of my errors, I was obliged to make subsequent revision.

We shook hands formally and she gave me a timid, tangential smile, but did not speak nor rise nor make any further attempt at communication; she just went on sitting there, quietly and primly perched on the chair, looking down at her nails, most of which were badly gnawed – and waiting for me to conduct the meeting as I saw fit.

No easy task, this. It was like dealing, not so much with a person as with an animal – no, better still, a bird. Yes, that is what she reminded me of – a bird, a funny little ruffled, migrating bird come briefly to rest; not exactly shy or frightened, but waiting and watchful – decidedly wary, and decidedly alien. I could discern no link with the excited voice which had filtered the shower of questions at me through a velvet bag on our previous encounter, nor did she tally with any of the images I had conjecturally formed. She was not monstrous, not ugly nor beautiful, and, except for the hair, not in any way remarkable. Jitters's terse description had been in fact a full one, and precise; there was not much of her and what there was was not much to look at. As yet there did not seem to be much to talk to either.

I cleared my throat and asked rather too loudly whether she was agreed on the bicycle ride. She nodded back politely, and then she raised her eyes to mine for the first time. They were dark, narrow and slanting, not at all birdlike and not at all shy; and having met mine with a frank, level stare, they ranged over my person from head to foot and then from foot to head again, displaying nothing other than well-disposed interest. In retrospect, I think it must have been this first direct encounter of eyes that marked the beginning of the gradual process of reassessment which was to culminate later on in my finding her little short of beautiful.

When we found the spare bike, it turned out to be much too high for her and much too rusty to alter, so we ended up by walking hesitatingly round the pond, still uncomfortably silent and uncomfortably aware – at least I was – of the rawness of my initial proposal to have a philosophical chat together. To philosophise alone was, I felt, in itself a delicate enough proceeding, comparable to the rearing of an exotic plant in an unsuitable environment; to do so *à deux* a yet more artful cultivation that must grow imperceptibly slowly on a rich soil of mutual understanding and intellectual sympathy; whereas to sit solemnly down with a total stranger – particularly one as distant as this – and say 'Now, let's talk philosophy' seemed to be as lethal to the issue as is the abrupt baring of the genitals to a strategic seduction. I began sorely to regret my suggestion.

At the far end of the **pond there** was a ramshackle wooden construction, half in half out of the water, which looked as if it had once served as a boat-house. It afforded little comfort, at best shade and partial privacy, but it was here that we eventually squatted down for the impending discussion which Martina's silence – benign but weighty – was beginning to turn into such a grossly artificial enterprise. So far, except for a squeal of dismay when trying to stride the bicycle, not a sound had come from her, and now that we had reached a comparative destination, all she did was to sit down quietly and gaze at the scummy surface of the water, her body curled gracefully inside the bulky sack of her clothing, seemingly and annoyingly quite at her ease.

Close to exasperation, I tried a traditional opening. 'What branch of philosophy are you interested in?' I asked.

'Branch?' she said seriously, not taking her eyes off the pond. 'Not branches, really . . . If anything I am interested in roots.' Then she relapsed into silence.

'Ah!' I said awkwardly. This was at least a response, but it was hardly more encouraging than her silence. I shifted my position and took to watching her closely: underlying her apparent absorption in the midges I thought I could begin to note a certain consciousness of my presence. If she was so unversed in conventional methods for getting the conversational ball rolling – as someone might well be who has lived a great slice of their life in solitary confinement, I allowed – then I too could waive them for the time being; and I decided to sit there likewise, staring at her staring at the pond, until she made some effort towards a more recognisable form of sociability. A few minutes passed.

When she spoke, however, I realised that my pique was wasted: she had been silent because still seriously considering my question and intent on giving it a well-thought-out answer. 'Ontology, therefore,' she said, as if no interval had elapsed between premise and conclusion, and waited again calmly for my next move.

'And logic?' I inquired, a trifle woodenly and still under the sway of considerable embarrassment.

'Logic? Well, logic . . . ' she began thoughtfully, again taking my wide, phatic question at face value and blithely unaffected by my unease, 'that's a mean question, you know. A tricky one. It needs a long answer.' She raised her eyebrows at me seeking my permission to continue, as if she knew from experience how easy it was for her to bore people on this subject.

'Go ahead,' I nodded and ahead she went. Slowly and

clearly, and, I may add, without boring me for one single instant, she began to expound to me her views on the nature of logic: its status within philosophy proper, its scope, utility, history, its claims and limitations. My embarrassment and my misgivings might never have existed. The more she spoke the further they receded, until I was unaware of anything other than the strict content of what she was saying. I had been unprepared for a competence of this kind. Her opinions were fresh and unorthodox and widely divergent from my own; the train of her thought, which I can only describe as a kind of scrupulously sustained irrationalism rationally argued for every step of the way, proved an irresistible combination of the unacceptable and unanswerable. Never had I enjoyed myself so thoroughly and so unpredictably; it was in fact not until I got bitten on the wrist by a particularly persistent gnat that I gave a glance at my watch and realised we had spent the best part of two hours in unflagging discussion. I got reluctantly to my feet and explained about the pressures of my time-table.

'Perhaps we could meet again here tomorrow?' I suggested, remembering suddenly that I had asked her none of the questions about her personal plight which had earlier on seemed so compelling and important. I had in fact done little else except pick her brains; and quite rapaciously too, seeing that they were worth the picking and provided a welcome change after Frogface's baskets-ful of beans. I had done nothing to try and find out whether she was contented or miserable, resigned to her narrow fate or yearning for that kind of existence which is normally granted to a quick-witted, presentable girl of her age. In short, I had behaved so far very selfishly.

'Tomorrow you could tell me a little about yourself,' I added. The long eyes looked at me, narrowing shrewdly until reduced to two dark slits, and she said almost angrily,

'Don't spoil things, Ludwig, please. I thought I had made it clear to you I don't need a doctor. If we are to be friends then you must forget about your profession and ask me no questions about myself. I am what I think. Can't that be enough to start with?'

'That's a very ridiculous way of putting it,' I said hotly, trying to digest her rebuff and not wholly succeeding. 'I might just as well say that you are what I think; and I think, Martina,' here I checked myself and chose my words carefully so as not to scare her further away, 'I think you are a very pretty,' this was not yet true, 'very fascinating,' this was, 'girl who is leading an unnecessarily ugly life. Why, I don't know, and if you don't want to tell me then I don't even want to know; but I do want to make sure it becomes a little less ugly while I am here and have some say in the matter. I want to winkle you out of your tower for a bit – there'll be ample opportunity for you to crawl back there when I am gone – and I want . . .'
I tried to think of something that would sound friendly without being interfering. 'I want to cut your hair for you.' It came out with great conviction as I had just discovered that I truly did, and struck exactly the right note. All caginess disappeared immediately and she asked in excitement, 'You do? You want to cut my hair? When? Can you cut hair? Properly, I mean? Oh, Ludwig! Really?'

I had to damp her enthusiasm a bit and admit that I had never done it before. 'But I can do most things I put my mind to,' I reassured her. 'I shall have my own cut first and make a point of noticing how it's done.'

'Then it will be a man's haircut. I shall look like a man.'

I studied her carefully, making due allowances for the shapeless perimeter. 'No, I don't think you will,' and I smoothed back the springy tufts of red matting to reveal a small but well-proportioned oval, pale skin, unblemished save for a few freckles, sound teeth a little on the yellow side, and a fine, straight nose. I was close enough to taste her breath and to notice that it was clean-tasting and truffly. 'No, I don't think you will at all.'

'Good. See you tomorrow then, Ludwig. Bring the scissors by all means, but no stethoscope.'

The haircut turned out to be a more powerful ruse than I had intended. Its material effects were drastic enough, for my inexpertise led to my cutting off far more than either of us had intended, and Martina's head emerged from the shearing more birdlike than ever; there was indeed hardly anything left but a red, shiny cap. I thought it a great improvement – not as stylish as I had hoped, but no longer clumsy either: 'arresting' was perhaps the best way to describe it.

Its psychological effects on the other hand were nothing short of shattering. For what it did was to forge a first bond of physical intimacy between us – oh! the symbols that are covertly written into a pair of cleaving scissors and the falling of surrendered locks – which from that moment onwards drew us closer and closer, more and more rapidly, into a vortex of proximity bordering on symbiosis. What I mean, of course, to put it in those facile, hazy terms which I find so difficult to use after a lifetime spent chasing after precision in meaning at any stylistic price, is that we fell in love.

I trimmed her hair, she trimmed my beard; I bared the contents of my brain to her and was sincerely convinced that she did likewise. We argued and laughed and talked and were silent in a giddy progression of convergence, the intensity of which seemed to surprise us not one jot. We spent hours and hours knitting our thoughts together like a pair of industrious *tricoteurs*, to form what seemed to me not mere sums of stitches but products and powers. We sought each other's company avidly and outspokenly on every possible occasion, and even the fact that I had given up at her request all attempts at extracting information from her about the problematic areas of her past and present hardly constituted at that stage an appreciable barrier. I did not even, come to think of it, curb my questioning out of fear of upsetting her, nor from lack of interest, but I did so merely because I could somehow sense perfectly clearly that she was to all relevant purposes happy and free.

Yes, that is indeed the best way of putting it: we were in love. Or I was in love, to be more exact. And perhaps the expression is not such a hazy one after all. The proposition 'in' conveys very well the idea of complete immersion in a state so that any getting beyond it or outside it to have an impartial look at what is going on, becomes an impossibility. There is no meta-state, so to speak, no metastasis; and to labour the consideration a little further, one could even maintain that the popular misconception of love's blindness arises from this very source: it is not that those in love cannot see, it is that they cannot find a place to see from, for such a vantage point simply does not exist.

How did things look to me then, from the inside? And, if as insider I could not get out for the purpose of seeing, could I now as outsider ever hope to get in? Particularly as an outsider who had only been there once, and agonisingly briefly such a long time ago?

At this point, I, the unhappy and bewildered Professor Ludwig of later years, was obliged to take another rest from my journey into the past. It was so painful trying to remember the happiness I must then have felt and gradually coming to realise that, try as I might, I was only capable of calling up what philosophers nowadays call 'propositional' knowledge about it. I could, that is, make statements to myself about how I had felt; could tell myself for example that I had felt elated, had carried out my work with enthusiasm and a resident smile on my face which no amount of contrariety ever managed quite to erase; that in this strange phase of elation I took the stairs four, five at a time, found all the nuns suddenly charming, and went about my toilet with the solemnity of a religious rite; that I could feel at all times a kind of melting process going on in my loins that seemed curiously generative of my mental buoyancy; that I woke each morning with the single-minded joy of a child, the thought of Martina swinging into my awareness like a floodlight, illuminating every insignificant detail and charging it with import. I could tell myself all these things, know too that they were true representations of my state at that time and yet fail completely to grasp their meaning: some necessary ingredient for this had gone for ever, leaving me with nothing but cold little snippets of factual information. How it had really felt, what had made me bound up and down the stairs like that, laugh, whistle, sing, and ride the world like an ace of the surfboard, was as hidden and inaccessible now as knowledge of an unvisited world.

Yes, it was right here, in the inaccessibility of my memories rather than in the actual memories themselves, that the pain lay. I began wearily to complete my preparations for the coming night: I carried the empty tray out into the corridor, paid a visit to the bathroom, and spent some time there looking at my face in the mirror, every neuron in my brain straining to recapture just one moment's reflection of my past self. How often must a then young and high-spirited Ludwig have looked into the selfsame glass, sprucing himself up, trying to obliterate a pimple, making sure his beard was free of crumbs, clipping the hairs from inside his nostrils, performing countless other small attentions in order to improve himself humbly for his beloved.

'You were in love, Ludwig,' I told the very different face confronting me, and it stared uncomprehendingly back.

4

How much my state was evident to outside observers, I do not really know. My evenings with Father Hugh continued on much the same lines as before: sometimes Martina would accompany me there, sometimes I would go alone. If the latter then I would take her arguments along with me in her stead and bring them out tenderly and proudly with a comforting sense of re-establishing contact with her. If she were with me then I would let her do most of the talking, and sit back with my beer, watching across the top of the foam her intense, shorn head with its long, dark fissures of eyes shimmering with intelligence and amusement.

Funnily enough, Hugh was at first so nervous in her presence that she would often decline to come out of sympathy, and reluctance to upset him further. I put it down to the fact that he did not like women generally, but Martina, who did not herself seem at all surprised or put out by his reactions, would state quite simply and objectively, 'No. It's not that at all. It's just that he doesn't like me,' and would give a small shake of her head in resignation.

Gradually, though, he seemed to become more accustomed to her presence – indeed she was so bereft of self-consciousness and possessed so genuine a desire to be assessed on her utterances alone, that it was hard not to be drawn into conversation with her – and would settle down quite comfortably to his evening sessions with us both. I noticed, however, that he was more at ease on those evenings when the weather would constrain us indoors: outside, and especially as the light diminished, I could often catch him watching Martina with his typical blend of sadness and anxiety; and if, as sometimes happened, she challenged him to a game of chess, his concentration on the board was nullified by the watch he seemed compelled to keep upon his opponent's face. He never won once as far as I can remember, although he was by far the more experienced player.

The nuns, apart from their initial curiosity, which they managed partially and quite gracefully to conceal, at seeing Martina going out and about after so long a period of retirement, seemed tolerant and unsurprised. Most of them had paid her the odd visit now and then: Whiskers, of course, had procured her reading matter; Pinhead had collected her laundry; Simper (Zoë the seamstress) had at one time attempted to teach her to embroider; Jaundice had succeeded, where the other had failed – in teaching her to knit. I think that most of them were really quite fond of her, treating her more as a wayward pet than as a human being. In this they reminded me of those strait-laced owners of incompatibly lustful animals who grant their pets any amount of indulgent licence; and perhaps, like the pet owners, they drew from her a form of vicarious gratification, or else did not consider her to be bound by their more exacting moral code. Anyway, no eyebrows were raised, no wimples crinkled, by the spectacle of our constant companionship. I think in a way they were even relieved at having the responsibility of Martina's entertainment – or, less ambitiously, for the filling-in of her unlimited spare time – taken off their hands for a while. The only attentive and preoccupied observer was Frogface. She would summon me to her stuffy little cubby-hole regularly twice a week, and would subject me to microscopic study through her pink lenses, ostensibly inquiring after Martina's overall welfare; was she 'coming out of herself' now a little more? We seemed to be getting on famously, was this thanks to our mutual interest in 'things philosophical'? Was she perhaps getting – how should she put it – a little *too* attached to me? Had I considered that in less than two months' time Martina would be on her own again? (I had indeed not considered this last point, nor did I intend to, for I intimately knew that when I left, no matter how much resistance and how many bureaucratic or other difficulties I would have to overcome to achieve this, Martina would be coming with me.) These and similar questions Frogface bombarded me with continuously. It was ironic that the one question to which she most ardently desired an answer was the very one which she could not find a way, however roundabout, to ask: for she was, of course, consumed by curiosity as to whether I had slept with Martina, or, to put it more precisely, since it may well have been that the idea of a fully blown sexual relationship between us was to her blinkered mind inconceivable in its enormity, what the exact nature of our physical union was; how deep it was, how detailed and how daring. More ironically still, I do not know that I could have given her an answer. We had – or at least so it seemed to me during the first intoxicating stages of our involvement – already reached that degree of unison at which the question itself has become otiose. Chronologically, I suppose we had not yet formally completed the act of physical conjunction: the boat-house was too uncomfortable, the veiled, praying-mantis figures too omnipresent. But this was a contingent fact, whereas that it happen sooner or later was necessary. Perhaps I am not explaining this very well. What I mean is that after our minds – and our bodies too, for that matter, within the limits imposed by logistic constraints – had touched at most available spots, to attach, as Sister Lucy blatantly did, such significance to one specific modality of compenetration as opposed to others seemed to me at first amusingly naïve.

Poor Frogface, I thought to myself, as I watched her grappling like Julian with allusions and euphemisms, carrying the added handicap of a reputation for down-to-earth, spade-is-spade forthrightness which made her task doubly difficult; poor Frogface, your question is an unimportant one and has no answer anyway, beyond an uninformative 'yes and no'.

As the days wore on, however, and more especially as the nights did – nights largely spent wrestling with the problems imposed by my then young, fit and well-rested body which caused me a lot more clandestine laundering and a lot of regretful submission to the law of entropy (it was like having bottle after bottle of overflowing champagne – or, more modestly, beer – with no goblet to catch it in) – my cerebral smugness on this matter began to desert me.

Perhaps swayed by Frogface's unshakable belief in its primacy, perhaps spontaneously forced to re-estimate the strength of my body's anchorage in the temporal, to sleep with Martina, to lie with her naked on a proper bed, all hampering and dividing layers of clothing removed, to be able at last to peel all those abominable garments off her and disclose the sleek little white body inside, to make love to her indulgently slowly and watch the funny, slanted eyes glaze over unseeingly at the apogee of pleasure, all these things which come under the simple heading of copulation did in fact begin to seem of uncomfortably pressing importance.

In a way I was quite simply thrilled by the discovery of this urgency; in a way it surprised and worried me. I knew – at least I thought I knew – that there was plenty of time ahead of us. I also knew from our furtive fumblings in the boat-house – or thought I did again – that she had little or no previous experience in sexual matters. Her complete trust in me, the oneness of our desires and intentions, and her unconventional spontaneity wedded to an almost uncanny quickness in learning (I wondered why she should have failed where embroidery was concerned? No doubt Simper was a worse teacher than I and had the disadvantage of a much less engrossing subject), led her to undertake some quaintly rarefied practices, it is true, but none the less I could tell – and partly from their very inventiveness – that these were not the fruit of experience. Who but a neophyte, I reasoned, would think up the idea of sketching their partner's member and then become dismayed because half-way through the sketch they had to invert the drawing pad?

Starting from such premises – i.e. that time was available and advisable – why then could I not smother my desire for the present, bide my time, and be satisfied by the intensity of communion we had already reached? Why run the unnecessary and possibly self-defeating risk of discovery? The answer to that was simple: I found – and more especially after the sketching session – that I could wait no longer. So maybe Frogface had a point there after all, and the culminating act of intercourse has its own weight and its own compulsion which no amount of intellectualising can paraphrase out; maybe it was I who was being ultimately the naïve and prudish one; but I do think that my confusion over this matter depended in great part on the fact that none, absolutely none, of my previous experiences in this area seemed to have any bearing upon my relationship with Martina. There had been women, and now there was she. I had known women, had affairs with women – five in number, let me add, lest I give the mistaken impression of being a libertine – lain with them, lived with them (in two cases) been friends with them (again in two cases, though not the same two) and now I had come across Martina. Any know-how I might have accumulated in my dealings with the former was of no use to me here. Martina was in another category. Well might I say so now, with the clarity of hindsight; but it was, too, exactly what I felt at the time. She was a hitherto missing part of myself, my Aristophanic completion. And despite this, or because of it, or for a set of totally unconnected reasons, I wanted desperately, urgently, compellingly, irresistibly, to slip into her bed and into her body. I had not yet known her a month.

I hope I have managed to reconstruct how close we were, one to the other, and how sure I was, rightly or wrongly, of this mutual closeness. It came therefore rather as a shock to me to come up against an adamant refusal on Martina's part that I should brave the hazards of discovery and make a night visit to her turret.

We had been yet again conscripted for gardening work by Frogface and I put the suggestion to Martina as we stooped together over the regrettably fructiferous beans. Her complexion – always noticeable for its whiteness – turned ashen and she muttered a garbled pretext of procrastination; something to do with dates. I took it she was referring to her menstrual cycle and chided her that she should let such an insignificant matter as a perfectly banal physiological regularity come between us at a crucial moment of our relationship.

'Silly, silly Doctor Ludwig,' she whispered back

angrily – the truculent figure of Sister Lucy, churning beans into her apron pouch with Stakhanovistic speed, was coming rapidly within earshot – 'think whatever you like. You *cannot*, you *must* not come to my room at night. Not *now*.' Her teeth were clenched in earnestness and the vegetables in her hand were being twisted by her into a greeny pulp. 'I . . . You . . . Oh, please, Ludwig, *please*,' she faltered in a voice so distressed as to be hardly recognisable.

'I want you,' I whispered back, scarcely less distressed. 'I want you so badly I could scream it out here and now to the Frog!' Here Frogface waved at us encouragingly to speed up our task and I waved compliantly back. 'But I shall never – *never*, do you understand, Martina, do anything you don't want me to. Only the thing is, I think you *do* really want . . . ' By now, though, Frogface had got so close that I could do nothing but stifle my words and my exuberance for the time being, and make do with a resolution to apply further pressure on Martina that evening, on our way back from the Chaplain's, where we were due to have supper.

After my usual tidy-up in the library – I had been rehauling amongst other things the philosophical section in search of works on logical neo-positivism which I was anxious for Martina to read, but which so far she had received warily, saying that her German was not up to it – I changed, regretting for the twentieth time having brought so few clothes, and ran downstairs and out into the scented evening air, pervaded by a sense of confident and almost total well-being. The moon would be nearly full by now, I reflected, so we could look forward to a long, relaxed, out-of-door chat and a bout of concerted Jitter-baiting; an activity which all three of us enjoyed, the bait only a trifle less than ourselves.

But when I reached the presbytery I could see that

Hugh did not share my exalted mood. He was sitting indoors, not out as I had expected to find him in such clement weather, and was huddled under one of the inhospitable horse-blankets, looking tired and cold. He told me at once that Martina had sent word she would not be coming.

'I'll go and see if I can persuade her to change her mind,' I volunteered eagerly. 'She won't want to miss a night like this. Unless,' I added, realising that our host was possibly feeling the effects of his illness, 'unless, that is, you would rather be alone, and have a bit of a rest from us for a change?'

He corrected me hurriedly, 'Lord, no, Wiggie! Only I'd prefer it to be just the two of us tonight, if you don't mind.' I did; but smiled and said nothing. Hugh was not talkative that evening, and he was off the beer. He tried a cigarette after our meal, but I could see he had no relish in it, and he stubbed it out almost immediately. I, on the other hand, drank and smoked liberally in order to keep the conversation flowing and to fill in the gap caused by Martina's absence. With uncharacteristic formality Hugh asked me to tell him of my childhood and I embarked without enthusiasm on this subject – not one I would myself have chosen to entertain a sick man. When I went to the kitchen to fill up my glass, I noticed with displeasure that not much effort was being made by the nuns towards their priest's housekeeping: the sink was sticky and beringed, the floor greasy. I wondered what his own childhood had been like, and what set of circumstances had led him to this ignominious and comfortless terminus as spiritual drone to a hive of bustling black and white bees. It seemed a little tactless though to play his own question back at him, so I continued to talk unwillingly about my own vicissitudes. In order to cheer him up, and to lighten the atmosphere a little, I told him

94

first of the chess sessions with my uncle in the Café Mozart – one of the few things I looked back on with undivided pleasure – and then of my brother's and my dabblings in psychic research, and how we had once tried to call up the ghost of Euclid to chivvy him over his fifth postulate: the glass we used for this purpose, a very valuable one, had spun out on the table in increasingly large triangles until it had bounced right off and had shattered at our feet, procuring us a well-deserved punishment for presuming to taunt the great geometer. The point Jitters drew was however a different one: 'Never go joking with the supernatural,' he said seriously. 'If there are ghosts – and who are we to say that there are not – they must be poor, lost things. Out of place and lonely. Doesn't do to go making fun of them.'

I gave a tolerant but irritated smile. It was, I reckoned, time to be getting back. He knew my opinions on superstition well enough by now surely; such a maudlin reaction could only be intended as provocation, and I was not falling into any such trap. To offset my crossness and my early departure, however, I took his hand – thin and shaky as a sparrow – in mine for a moment, disregarding the English habit of rationing one handshake per head per lifetime. He really did not look at all well. I hoped he was indeed getting the necessary medical attention.

'G'night, Wig,' he said, moved I think rather than otherwise by the contact of hands. 'One thing I wanted to say, before you go. If I were you I'd leave Martina be for a couple of days. Just a few days, you know. Nothing more. A couple of days. Three at the most.'

He seemed painfully embarrassed. No wonder, I thought. This was worse than the Hebrew taboos of the Old Testament. Why in the world should a Catholic priest of the twentieth century meddle in such matters?

Then suddenly a much more unpleasant thought came to me, which caught me with a kind of thud in the back of my throat. 'She told you to tell me that!' I said accusingly. 'She doesn't want to see me. Then she could have told me so herself, couldn't she? She knows I would never go against her wishes. Why didn't she tell me so herself?' More than anything I was stung by her having had recourse to an intermediary.

Jitters was silent; his embarrassment had not subsided. Slowly and half-heartedly he began weaving further jumbled explanations, but I held up my hand to stop him. I was not interested in what he might or might not say. I wanted to hear it straight from Martina.

Murmuring what I hoped sounded like acquiescence, I completed my leave-taking and returned to the main house, making as I did so a complete round of the building to see who, if anyone, was still awake.

The kitchen garden with its stark geometrical lay-out looked more like a war cemetery than a garden in the strong moonshine. A couple of lights were still on at the back, and Martina's thin, arched windows were dully illuminated. I let myself in and went straight to her turret: I was no longer worried, at this stage in our relationship, about being found talking to her, even at such a late hour, and my patience was – for reasons I have already explained – wearing a little thin.

As I drew near, I could however discern a low rhythmic murmur. It might of course have been her wireless which I knew she often listened to while reading, saying that it was less distracting than the silence, but there was such an odd droning quality in the voice that I instinctively checked my pace and began to edge my way through her perennially untidy bathroom with extreme caution. Instead of calling out her name or trying to attract her attention, I put my eye to the keyhole, as I had done on the very first occasion and had a preliminary peer through. Not so much surprise as sheer anger surged through me at what I saw. The scene was not very different from what it had been then: Martina was sitting as before at the table, dressed in her skimpy tartan dressing-gown, with her head inserted in the atrocious velvet bag. On the opposite side of the table, though, there sat another figure. It was Frogface – uncharacteristically subdued – who appeared to be reading aloud to her some repetitive devotional work. Each single sentence was uttered with the same plaintive cadence, and was punctuated from the next by a low, monotonous 'Ora pro nobis'.

I was offended both for and by Martina. How could she, I asked myself angrily, sit there passively with that degrading sack hiding her beautiful head; hiding her beautiful eyes that I was used to watch shining with energy – assessing, watching, judging? How could she sit there blindfold listening to this dirge of cumbrous church-Latin? And how dare Frogface inflict this ridiculous, time-wasting torment on her? How dare the nuns countenance – encourage even – her pathetic mania for self-denial and self-abasement? Surely they would have been wiser to have called in a professional psychotherapist than mess about with her in this inadequate, incompetent and cruel way?

I longed to batter on the door, to call her name, to burst into the stuffy, dark room, so filled with the sound of the stale Latin words that they seemed to hover in the air like the cloying fumes of incense, and to take her into my arms and comfort her and strip the hideous covering from her face – and from her body too, for that matter. She did not even need a psychiatrist, I told myself; she needed me, and me alone. And yet she had refused to see me that evening, and had chosen instead the company of Sister Lucy and this mournful, threnodic mumble of litanies.

I stood trembling, with my outspread hands pressed against the door, uncertain of what I was to do, uncertain even of my own feelings.

I felt above all else an overwhelming sense of betrayal, but not yet of loss. I should have realised, I thought, that the impression of union which I had so strongly experienced had been necessarily delusive. Martina's refusal to discuss the past had not been, as was mine, a result of complete and perfect absorption in the present. My arrival had accomplished no fairy-tale awakening, as I had been foolish and presumptuous enough to assume. She was, on the contrary, still as fast imprisoned as on the night I had first seen her, and whether by imaginary or real fetters made little difference – they were either way of her own making. Or were they? Hugh had not explicitly stated that she herself had refused to come; she had 'sent word' – that might mean anything. The sense of normality which Frogface had managed to convey to me in our talk among the tombstones I now saw could easily have been illusory. Martina's refusal to discuss anything that touched – however remotely – upon the subject of herself could equally be dictated by fear, not of the past, but of the present. Perhaps my first hunch had been right after all; perhaps she was indeed being detained against her will. Perhaps she had not chosen Frogface's company after all, but it had been forced on her. I stooped down to the keyhole once more, and may have made a noise with my hands as I did so, for when I looked once more into the dimly lit turret the goggles, disconcertingly glazed with light so that the head which wore them took on an amphibian aspect worthy of my nickname and of my most hysterical suspicions, were staring straight at the door, their reading interrupted.

I began stealthily to back away, not before noticing however one further detail which not only confirmed these suspicions but also annihilated whatever hopes I had had of getting any sleep that night: Martina's hands, lying patiently joined on the table before her, were bound at the wrists.

Next day I worked hard and blindly all morning. What sleep I had managed to get had been blighted by dreams of such immediate functionality as to need no symbolic dress and had given me scant refreshment – Martina bound and gagged; Martina in chains with Frogface standing over her brandishing a pair of gigantic knitting-needles; myself wedged in the narrow turret window unable to wriggle either backward or forward. I was angry, worried and tired. Before lunch, therefore, and before my anger could be even minimally blunted by the ingestion of food, I stalked determinedly to Frogface's hideout under the stairs. There was no question this time of choosing a suitable moment, and it was only a fastidious reluctance to waste one penny of the nuns' wretched money that kept me in check until the one o'clock bell rang.

I knocked perfunctorily and entered without waiting for an answer. The room was empty – or rather the cupboard was, for you could hardly call it a room – and I was about to resume my search for its tenant, still sustained by a reckless surge of righteousness, when I remembered what Sister Lucy had said about the documents which had accompanied Martina on her arrival and shut the door behind me quietly instead. She had said, had she not, that a medical report was in her possession and that I might peruse it should I wish? I felt therefore only the faintest echo of a qualm at what I was about to do; for there had, I told myself calmly, been prevarication enough as it was; it was time the much-called-for light from outside was let in.

Luckily it was not hard to find what I was looking for, as the bossy, energetic Sister kept her study as neatly and symmetrically as she did the garden; indeed, it was while I was thus thumbing through her papers that I first suspected she was the one in charge of plotting out the graveyard too – perhaps that was why she was so fond of it, I surmised: because it testified to her organisational skill, and because she could not only put people where she wanted them, but could also be sure they would stay there.

Squeezing my way round the writing table which occupied most of the space, I scanned the row of shelves behind. Each shelf was taped with a piece of sticking plaster, and an inky inscription stated the unifying criterion of its contents thus: 'Misc. Corresp.', 'Corresp. F.C.R.', 'Hort.hints', 'Work books 36–40', 'Hosp.', (I looked through one or two of these files, but found nothing of interest), 'Aliment.' – this was unexpected; it was surely more the Bursar's province, but then Frogface's stubby fingers seemed to be in a whole lot of pies – 'Household Manag.', and so forth, down to ground level. At the end of the second to bottom shelf, marked firmly 'Own stuff', I found what I was after: a slim, unmarked yellow folder, on the inside of which was carefully printed: 'Mart. W. Personal'. I gave a rapid glance at the contents: chiefly these seemed to be standard, typed-in forms of the refugee organisation reporting Martina's various transfers, with the usual rubrics for name, parentage, estimated age, place of origin – the bare data of which I was already in possession – followed by the addresses of the places to which she had been posted. Each form, varying in fact in this last particular only, ended with the brief comment: 'Allocation unsuitable.'

Next I skimmed through a batch of letters, apparently

from the families who had extended their hospitality towards her, stating their reasons for discontinuing it; once more there was almost unanimous recourse to the nebulous term 'unsuitable' or its cognates: 'We regret that Martina is unlikely ever to fit in with us here . . . ' 'My wife and I feel bound to admit that this particular charge is unable to adjust . . . ', etc., etc. One lady from Torquay had modified the theme somewhat by blaming herself for lack of adaptability; her letter was poorly phrased and written but it did not have the awkwardly reserved air of the others: 'I am now', it went, 'at my wit's end to know what to do about the child . . . no getting through to her . . . it is upsetting the others and my Marcus has not been right since she came.' She ended with nothing short of begging for Martina to be taken off her hands before – the letter went – 'she goes and does something worse'. Had my pity not been entirely for Martina I could have felt quite sorry for the poor thing. I was on the lookout for something more informative than these scanty missives, however, some of which did not even appear to be complete, and I leafed through them cursorily: Martina seemed to have stayed nowhere for more than a few weeks and to have bounced back to the organisation with disconsolate regularity. My heart went out to her in sympathy – no wonder she had become so reticent about her past; reticence, I realised, must have come to constitute a necessary form of self-defence after the sustained shuttlecock saga of her childhood.

Hearing a booted footfall on the stairs above, I paused for a moment in my reading, then I resumed unperturbed, remembering my wrath. Let the Frog come; let her find me rifling her papers without explicit consent. If she so much as dared to voice an objection, I would give her – and gladly – a vituperative piece of my mind. Perhaps I might even go so far as to threaten legal intervention in defence of Martina's rights. Things, I felt, were coming to a head, or if they weren't then they certainly should be and I myself would see to it that they did.

After the letters came a medical report. I wiped my spectacles over with a handkerchief in preparation – this might well be what I was looking for.

But no. Here again was the terse official form – age, height, weight, colour of eyes, distinguishing marks; 'none' I read wryly, thinking that I could myself distinguish her body in a multitude, even without my glasses. Physical desire invaded my pelvic region like a spreading wine-stain, and I sat down in Frogface's chair to allow it to ebb, reflecting how unaccustomed the chair must be to such inflamed tenure; then, with a further polish to my glasses which had misted over once more, I went back to the forms. The space for anamnesic data had hardly been used at all, and this, familiar as I was with Martina's taciturn memory, did not surprise me; what did surprise me was that such a negative fact had not in itself been queried. Past disturbances, for example, was followed by the placid comment: none. Infectious diseases: none. Surgery: no. Hereditary illnesses: a question mark. Living relatives: another question mark. Mental disturbances: here the comment exceeded the monosyllable by a relatively wordy 'see overleaf' referring the reader to the next page which was headed promisingly 'Psychiatrist's Report', but I could see at a glance that it was not going to be of much use to me: a compact four lines of reassuring but trivial remarks on Martina's unexceptionable state of psychic welfare 'despite the harrowing nature of recent experiences the patient has undergone'. I was about to close the folder and replace it from where I had taken it, when I noticed a sheet of royal blue notepaper tucked into a flap on the inside cover: not a sheet, in fact, for there were three sheets – amazingly closely written,

102

horizontally and vertically crossed in paper-saving zeal and in the blackest of inks, making the pages seem stiff and solid, like pieces of curiously hectic and funereal wickerwork.

Not anxious to spend more time than necessary in Lucy's airless cubby-hole, this letter I pocketed and went to the guest refectory for my solitary luncheon. I was always quick over it, but on this occasion it took me four minutes flat and tasted of nothing at all.

Alone once more in my turret, I fished out the blue pages and began carefully to plough my way through the wilderness of words. Once I got the hang of it and was able to disregard the message running at right-angles to the one I was deciphering, I found I could read it fairly easily, becoming however increasingly disquieted by what I read.

The writer, I judged, must be a professional psychotherapist – most likely an analyst – but was writing in an unofficial capacity, not to the organisation itself but to one of the members occupying some key position there. 'My dear Giles,' it began, 'Carrying out the request you made to me at our last meeting, I have so far had three orientative sessions with Miss W. Owing to the brevity of these encounters and to the scarcity of material I was able to extract, I beg of you to consider my opinion as tentative and fallible to a high degree.' Ha! I thought to myself; here we go with the ritual prelude to dogmatic balderdash – 'Unfortunately, as I believe I also made quite clear to you from the start, prior commitments render any further consultations impossible. There is, you realise, no question of the financial aspect bringing its weight to bear. I am quite simply overworked. I mentioned the case to Simone at your suggestion but her situation is as – if not more – impossible than mine. If this atrocious holocaust does not come to an end soon we

103

shall all need treatment of some kind or other. Forgive me if I am letting you down over this. I cannot do otherwise. *Re* the little Miss W . . . '

Here I had to twist the page round and the writing became more difficult to follow, some words I could hardly make out at all.

Re the little Miss W . . . *Re* the little Miss W . . . I read on in growing anxiety. The analyst in his three brief sessions had certainly formed, however tentatively and fallibly, both decided and drastic opinions: 'It is my belief', ran one line, 'that the patient is affected by acute and irreversible paranoia, likely to prove destructive of her own psychic equilibrium and that of others . . . ' and, further, 'I cannot', the following word – presumably an adverb – was impossible to decipher, 'recommend any – blur – therapy than segregation in order to curb the more macroscopic brand of damage that may result. Despite the gravity of traumas sustained and taking into account the age of the patient and the apparent quality and resilience of her intellectual apparatus when unaffected by delirium, I strongly advise against institutionalisation if it is in your power to achieve this and if there is any alternative way of ensuring a desired maximum of safety. *That* way indeed, my dear Giles, madness lies. I recently had a case . . . '

Two pages followed describing the plight of some poor, crazed patient of his who, as far as I could make out, was under the impression – much as are the subjects of worn and widely circulated jokes on lunatics but never to my knowledge people in everyday life – that he was some kind of animal. The digression seemed to me out of place and in bad taste; I could not see what pertinence it could have to Martina's story of loss and deprivation through the cataclysm of war, nor why he was devoting so much space to it. Most likely it was, I thought, a kind of professional showing off: look what a mess this one was in, and look how I sorted him out. He had refused to take on Martina, though, which made me feel quite proud of her. She had evidently flummoxed him properly: outwitted him. My clever, adored Martina; what torment she must have gone through with these blundering and self-opinionated know-alls.

'Episode A,' the letter continued, 'if indeed it *was* A, was unavoidable; episode B perhaps likewise. C could and should have been circumvented. There must be no D.' (This was underlined twice). 'Forgive me if . . . etc., etc. . . . ' The closing rigmarole ended verbosely much as it had begun with weak claims to defeasibility, excuses for the failed co-operation, and with reiterated insistence on Martina's removal from society.

Well, it looked as though the psychoanalyst's advice had been taken, and in earnest. Martina had been shut away now for years, following the 'tentative and fallible' opinion of someone who had briefly interviewed her years ago in a purely unprofessional capacity and had pronounced her as suffering from a dangerous and irreversible (irreversible – the arrogance of that judgment!) form of paranoia. He had branded her as mad. Dangerously mad. And what is more it looked as if his label had stuck. Perhaps she had even been influenced by it herself, I realised, but then surely not so far as to be totally taken in by him. She loathed and mistrusted doctors – that in itself seemed a healthy enough reaction, but she had been pitted against this one, and on her own admission against others too, when still a mere child. How could she have helped but fall victim, at least partially, to their suggestions? Things now began to take on a clearer shape in my mind, and I sat down on the edge of the bed and began to set them out in a more methodical fashion.

On Martina, for reasons that were not yet clear to me but which in their precise form and details were of no particular interest or import at this stage – there would be plenty of time for us to face the unravelling of these deep-rooted problems together, I decided, when I had succeeded in prising her out of her isolation and taking her away with me to Salzburg, or to Vienna, or to London, or wherever we chose to make our home – an irresponsible and wantonly superficial judgment of insanity had been passed. This judgment what is more had been widely and enduringly accepted, not only by those who surrounded her but perhaps even, and understandably, by Martina herself. In this light a lot of hitherto perplexing facts began to fall into perspective: if Martina played the lunatic, then it was Sister Lucy who had cast herself in the role of confidante-cum-warder; the Reverend Mother saw herself as legally responsible for a potentially dangerous charge; while the community in general treated her with gentle forbearance, placing their trust in the efficacy of prayer alone for her recovery combined with such well-tried palliatives as knitting, sewing and basket-weaving; along the same trite lines perhaps they even considered that a little amorous dalliance would prove distracting and beneficial. Jitters – still greater victim of popular superstition – was scared stiff of her, his fear being heightened by the added factors of darkness and the phases of the moon. No wonder he couldn't concentrate on his game of chess! The moon, yes, the moon. This played a part in Martina's own fears and phobias too; regrettable in one so sceptical and so well-read, but there again understandable. Scepticism, after all, is only tenable in the abstract. My poor little love. So that was why she chased her head into a velvet bag at every full moon! She was afraid of herself. And that was why she balked at seeing me at night: it was not that she did not love me, did not desire me – no, she was frightened of harming me. And that too was why she suffered herself to be fettered to a chair and exorcised by Latin ritual. The picture began to crystallise. I was – we both were – surrounded not by a planned conspiracy of any kind but by a web of hysterical superstition and by a mountainous quantity of downright, ignorant stupidity.

I got to my feet feeling enlightened and relieved but at the same time even more angry than formerly, and pacing round the restricted space I began to meditate on the best course of action. Things had to be righted somehow, and a few silly myths exploded; but not, if possible, with too violent a report lest my poor, bewildered love take fright and crawl back for protection into the narrow but safe prison which she had made for herself over the years.

My anger was principally directed now against Frogface. For Martina I could make so many allowances – she was after all fighting to preserve her sanity, even if this paradoxically entailed posing as a lunatic. Starting from her handicapped draw as orphaned and destitute child-refugee, and stultified by God knows what traumatic wartime experience, she had at least found herself a quiet, comfortable little niche from which to carry on the only pastime which interested her – her readings in philosophy. Free food, free lodging, clothes (such as they were), an unoppressive society and reading matter *ad libitum*, these were amenities scarcely to be sniffed at by one in her position. It was up to me to show her what else the world had to offer, and I was sure I had already succeeded in giving her a first, pleasurable taste. The prising, I decided happily, would have to be swift and predominantly physical.

Frogface, though, was another matter. No allowances

could be made for her. Far from trying to cure Martina of her delusions, she was encouraging and abetting them, going so far in her bossiness and love of domination as to sit down and play lunatics along with her. I wondered if the Convent's medical adviser had any inkling of what was going on, and whether it was my duty to contact him, but I decided that this could only produce the undesired effect of putting Frogface on her guard and of upsetting Martina, who surely was entitled at long last to recognition as a free agent and to a dose of straight dealing – decisions regarding her having been taken up to now behind her back, above her head, everywhere except right in front of her where they should have been. Firstly I would concentrate on forging as strong a physical bond between us as I was able – I should have to wait until the critical lunar phase had passed for this, which was irritating, but I had waited so long already and the following period would be none the less agreeable for the delay; secondly, having won her confidence and her allegiance, I would openly discuss with her the secret of her so-called madness, and convince her she need no longer gain purchase on the world by means of this expedient, and that henceforth I would provide a world for her. I would coax her back to normality by the sheer force of my faith in her. Never, never for one instant did I doubt her sanity, nor my own capacities of conviction. It might prove tricky, of course, but it was supremely possible – rather like the netting of a bird: a beautiful, exciting, rare prize of a bird, where the strong, conclusive tug to the net must be given neither too soon nor too late; but I had no doubt either that I would win her in the end. I had not planned on taking up routine medical practice nor taking a wife, yet now it looked as if I was willingly headed for both courses. I went over to my cramped desk where my suspended studies were displayed: the opened pages were collecting already a thin film of dust. I closed the books with a gentle snap. No more of them for the present: first I must net Martina. There would be time for study later.

5

I gave her two days, or rather gave the moon two days to start its waning in earnest. I neither went to her turret, nor sent messages, nor tried to contact her in any way. I was sure she could not do without me for long, and I was right. On the third day after that disastrous evening when I had discovered her caught in Frogface's litanic spell, Martina emerged from the seclusion of her turret and came down to the library where I was working. She looked even paler than usual and very shamefaced. The sinews of my thighs weakened when I saw her enter; I wanted nothing so much as to give her the widest and most reassuring smile I could summon, but I remembered that from her angle I had been repulsed by her, ignored for the best part of three days, and been given no explanation or excuse as to why, so I managed instead to look reproachful and puzzled.

She came over to my desk and held out a hand, palm upwards, as if offering an inexistent but precious gift – everything and at the same time nothing. The hand shook slightly. 'I will come to Father Hugh's with you this evening. If you still want me to, that is . . . ' she began, but I put a finger to my lips – there was a nun helping herself to literature from one of the bookcases in a far corner – and encircled her skinny wrist.

'No!' I hissed at her in spurious fierceness but genuine emotion, 'that's not quite good enough, Martina. There are a few things we must tackle first, in private. I am coming to your room after lunch.'

It pained me to use crash tactics such as these but I felt the moment was propitious. Her hand was still extended like a small, unstable tray; the undefined offering held good; it was time to accept her excuses and her renewed friendship, and to exact much more besides. In retrospect, I can see that this was the crucial moment of my suit: it was then, when I sat holding her wrist in my hot, encompassing hand in a neatly inverted symbolisation of the sexual act of male possession, that my carnal knowledge of her – if so it can be termed – really began. The rest I accomplished, as I had warned or promised, and with singular lack of finesse, after lunch.

From then on it was as if a great weight had been taken from me: the first part of my plan had worked, and I was binding Martina to me closer and closer with every day that passed. The simile of removed weight is particularly apt: I leapt around quite literally, like a horse accustomed to leaden shoes that finds itself unexpectedly light-shod in aluminium; my intoxication returned and I raced up the stairs once more, slid down banisters, skated down the corridors, worked with speed and enthusiasm, and felt myself on the brink of constant amusement. I began to find the nuns as endearing as before – except for Frogface. I smiled at them all. I loved Jitters. I loved my evenings – our evenings – with him more than ever, and reached perhaps the closest distance to happiness that I have ever achieved when watching Martina frown over the chess board, crinkling her freckled nose in concentration, and knowing that we would shortly be engaged in a yet more exacting activity. We made love

111

twice, thrice daily, making no more than the most perfunctory efforts to formally cover our tracks. As I had predicted, the nuns, if indeed they suspected anything, were bent on toleration: perhaps my medical status gave them added reassurance. Here they misjudged me though, for not only had I seduced her under their very noses but I was moreover determined to make Martina pregnant. It was part of my welding strategy. A pregnancy would play heavily in my favour when the time came for taking Martina away – she could hardly have an illegitimate child in the Convent precincts, I reasoned. Besides, I wanted the child on genetic grounds also, for surely the odds were in favour of our breeding a genius, and not a bad-looking one either. Everything was running smoothly and according to plan: Martina was confident and happy, I was ecstatic, the nuns were complaisant, Jitters welcoming, and Frogface's sway usurped. It was, I felt, almost time to enter phase two of my courtship and admit to my knowledge of her . . . what could one call it? – her infirmity, her secret; time to make light of it with her, help her to do the same, and then go on to the sobering though delightful task of planning our future together.

I chose the moment carefully. Two weeks had now passed of total physical absorption one in the other, and we were beginning to surface and to find time to talk again; on this particular afternoon we were sitting by the edge of the pond eating chocolate biscuits which I had bought from the village shop. Well-wrapped goods were beginning to appear on the market and Martina was more taken by the silver paper than the biscuits; she was ironing it out meticulously with her thumbnail and making minute goblets. I took a piece from her, rolled it into a thin band and placed it on her finger.

'Liebling,' I said, smoothing it round the contours of

her thin, white finger with its grubby, bitten-down nail, 'don't you think it's time we did some serious thinking about our future together? You can't stay on here when I have gone, you realise that? I can't just go away and leave you here.'

'What do you mean, Ludwig?' she said very slowly, staring at her finger with the paper ring and frowning.

'I mean that I can't leave you here,' I repeated with equal slowness. 'I mean that you must come with me when I leave. It is all very simple, Martina, and there need be . . .' I was giving the words all the emphasis and deliberation of which I was capable. '. . . there need be no problems. No problems at all, unless, that is, we make them for ourselves.'

There was a long silence.

'You want me to marry you, Ludwig,' she said at length and with as much expression and surprise in her voice as if she were quoting an arbitrary proposition in one of her logical exercises, 'you want me to come and live with you.'

I sat quite still, holding my breath. Then, as she seemed to have nothing further to say, but just sat there staring listlessly at her own hand, I breathed again and began quietly to tell her that little I knew about herself and how doubly little all of it mattered to me. I began too to describe to her my own vision of our life together: we would, I thought – two uprooted Europeans with nothing more substantial than our wits to rely on – do better to remain in England. I would practise medicine privately, seeing that German-speaking doctors always seem to go down well with the credulous English public and especially with its richer members; she could aim at a job at a university, or could continue to pursue her studies as a side-line and take up translating work. She might do all three. True, it would be a bit of a struggle to begin with, but we would be together and happy, and both of us had experienced hardships that would make things seem light in comparison. On and on I went, and the more I talked the more real and feasible the picture seemed to become. I started imagining the clothes I would buy her with my first earnings, and the books: first on my list of priorities came a silk dressing-gown and the works of Karl Popper. The more animatedly I spoke, though, the deeper her immobility became; not, I slowly began to realise, because my enthusiasm was carrying her along with me, but because she was steeling herself not to listen. When she did move, it was to flick the slip of silver paper into the pond.

The gesture chilled me more than her silence, but it was not until I had taken her head between my hands and twisted it round to face me that a concrete possibility of failure occurred to me: failure which, I fully realised now, would entail the ruin of my future as well as hers. And I was right about this: it would be erroneous to say that I have never looked at another woman since, or whatever the saying is, but I have never since, and I say this quite truthfully, been able to look into one, or after one, or forward to one. With Martina I could have done all this. Could and should. My grievous fault is that I did not carry out the second disjunct: I did not look after her well enough. But how could I; how could I have done so then, when I do not know how to this day?

Her face was stiff with restraint, but despite this tears were coursing down her cheeks. As in her voice formerly, I could perceive there no flicker of expression – just a blank, wet, white face like a slab of marble in the rain. Its blankness unnerved me: if I had made a false step I must unmake it now by the sheer force of my affection.

I began murmuring her name time after time, cajoling her, calming her, kneeling before her to take her in my arms, but she fended me off with a kind of automatic rigidity. Then she began to speak again, in a voice thin and taut as a piece of twine.

I listened first in anguish as she explained to me the impossibility of her ever leaving the Convent or of leading the normal kind of middle-class married life I had prospected to her, then with genuine curiosity as she began to give the reasons for her refusal. I came close to experiencing actual relief when she stated with clipped, matter-of-fact precision:

'You are right, of course; I am not mad. I am as sane as most people. More lucid, anyway. The question of insanity simply does not arise. The trouble is, Ludwig, you know so little about me. You know you love me and you think that is enough. I too know that I love you, but I know – *I know* – that this is not enough.' She bit cruelly into her underlip. 'There is something I have to tell you . . . something very dreadful which will finish everything between us because you will not believe me' – she held her hand against my mouth to stop me intervening – 'but which I *have* to say. Now. So that you realise why any sort of life for us together would be impossible. I am not like other people. I am not what you think. I am . . . I am . . . '

Her face, so close to mine, was distorted with the sheer effort of speaking and with an emotion that appeared to be shame. I planted a kiss on the hand that was covering my mouth, encouraging her to continue, for it seemed that the moment of healthy catharsis had at last arrived. It was a good thing perhaps that my mouth was hidden by her hand, for when at last she blurted out to me her terrible secret, my first reaction – quite supplanting the anxiety and interest which had preceded it – was one of

115

tender and relieved amusement; Martina told me that she was a werewolf.

Martina thought she was a werewolf. So at last we were getting somewhere. Of all the things I had feared when she embarked on her confession this was the most innocuous. It was a form of madness, of course, and the psychoanalyst had seen more clearly than I thought – I now saw the point of his digression on the man who thought he was an animal – but mercifully it was going to be an easy one to cure. The kaleidoscopic image I had of her settled into a new, more luminous, and I thought definitive pattern: there was, as I had fundamentally known all along, despite the see-saw of suspicions I had entertained on Frogface's account and despite my tendency to blame the nuns for what Jitters called 'shady dealings', for the mere fact that they were nuns, no conspiracy against Martina that she herself did not originate and conduct. Frogface seconded her not out of bossiness, as I had feared, but out of simple ignorance as to how these sort of cases should be treated, and simple ignorance could likewise account for the attitude of the rest of the community – for surely none of them could be quite so preposterous as to think . . . Then I returned to Jitters, and yet another bit of puzzle slipped into the pattern, accomplishing yet another revelation. So *that* was what was wrong with Jitters: he seriously believed himself to be living cheek by jowl with a female were-wolf. My amusement turned into pure exhilaration.

In unbounded relief and gaiety I drew Martina towards me. I had enough presence of mind not to laugh outright, but my happiness must have infected her because she was no longer tense and let herself be wrapped in my arms where she lay quietly, crying into my shoulder. Good, I thought, so she trusted me. She loved me. I could feel both her trust and her love. It was all

116

going to be so easy from now on. The very magnitude of her delusion made it so spoofable and touching. I would have her right in no time at all, or to be more exact in . . . I calculated the days that separated us from the next full moon (the moon, of course; the velvet bag. Martina had been hiding her furry whiskers in a velvet bag! Oh, my poor, dear, rational little philosophess! The utter absurdity of the whole thing!) . . . in two weeks' time. No more shrouding nonsense; no more litanies. We would sit the night out together, she and I this time, and I would show her just how delightful I personally found lycanthropes – from the points of their ears down to the tips of their bushy tails. The difficulty – the only difficulty as far as I could see – lay in getting Martina herself to agree to such a trenchant cure. For the moment I said nothing, but went on cradling her in my arms. She was quite still now and was no longer crying. She trusted me. Everything would work out well.

My high mood of optimism, however, did not last. Martina met my concrete suggestions as to how we should take the wolf by the tail with nothing short of horror. Reverting to her thin, stringy voice, she told me flatly that sooner than allow me – me of all people – to watch with her on the night of the full moon, she would kill herself. I had been prepared for a refusal, but not such a final one as this, nor one which entailed a risk I could not possibly afford to run. In the following days therefore I set myself the urgent task of dismantling her resistance. Partly I resorted to a close, hammering form of philosophical argument in defence of the virtues she was most abusing: reason and common sense (and anyone who has had the least brush with philosophy will know how dull and difficult they are to defend); partly to a more light-hearted technique – that of werewolf-debunking, which consisted in growling and barking at Martina and wagging an imaginary tail, and so forth, until she was obliged to laugh, which in fact she often did.

Her refusal to co-operate remained however inflexible, and my efforts to bring her round were defeated or at least hampered by the difficulty I personally had – not in taking the situation seriously, nor in taking Martina seriously, for it was only too evident that she was in a certain sense gravely ill and only too clear to me that my whole life's happiness depended on her recovery – but in taking seriously the actual nature of her delusion. There were times when, knowing as I did the eclectic and brilliant quality of her mind, it seemed to me impossible that she should be truly victim of such a transparently ridiculous conviction. As I said, she too was capable of seeing the funny side of the whole affair and of laughing at my tactics of demystification. Once or twice I was on the point of calling up an acquaintance of mine who was a lecturer in psychology and of talking matters over with him, but on reflection it seemed to me unnecessary – for how could anyone succeed better than myself who was tied to Martina by a life-line of love and understanding? Yes, I knew perfectly well what was to be done and how to set about it – all that was lacking was Martina's consent to the decisive spoofing experiment.

As the days passed, however, I was forced to realise that I was making little progress in this direction. I spent more and more time with her to the detriment of my work in the library, although here, fortunately, I was already engaged on the finishing stages of organisation and reckoned that no one could accuse me of shirking; nor for that matter did I much care, when the other work I had to do was so infinitely more important.

There was, besides, another reason why my slacking-off and total engrossment in Martina were liable to be overlooked: the community had begun its annual 're-treat' – a period of ten days or so during which all external, material concerns were officially shelved in favour of intense spiritual introspection and meditation. The rule of silence was extended to cover twenty-three of the twenty-four hours; the nuns padded about in a more restrained fashion than their habitual stomping, spent a still greater deal of time in church, made a heavier run on pious literature, and conducted all their communication in their practised code of hand-signals.

To tell the truth, it took me a couple of days to notice these changes in tempo and intensity in the lives of the Sisters, absorbed as I was in my own activities, which included, of course, the demanding but peerless task of making love to Martina as often and as long as possible. I first noticed it indeed during this very act: it was early afternoon, the house and grounds so still that every noise we made seemed unusually magnified, and I had to stop Martina's mouth with my own – my hands were not available for this purpose, one being clasped over her nipple, the other imprisoned by the forefinger in her sphincter – to smother the moans she was making. She bit me then, I recall, with her small, creamy, all-too-human teeth, and I teased her about this afterwards. It was she who told me the reason for this intensified silence, but I would have cottoned on anyway independently the next day, for it was then that the spiritual director of the retreat arrived in person: none other than the author of the Convent's current number one favourite, Father Constantine Read.

Though conserving its formal curtain of silence, the whole place went into a turmoil. The morning saw terrific bustlings and preparations: blankets, quite unlike the coarse, rank variety reserved for Father Hugh, were

119

carried upstairs: sumptuous flowers appeared (goodness knows from where, considering the spartan and utilitarian character of the garden) and were taken in part upstairs to adorn, I suppose, the quarters of the illustrious author, in part to the church.

Later in the day I had a peep inside the building and noticed that they had rigged up a central lectern there and so weighted it down with blossoms that it looked more suited to a wedding address or to the awarding of prizes at a flower show. From my desk in the library I could observe a ceaseless passage between house and church: vestments were being ferried over – again larger and grander than those of the Chaplain – clean altar cloths, fresh candles, extra chairs and so forth, all carried by a stream of worker-nuns under the silent supervision of Frogface. The gardener was raking the gravel – the only time I ever saw this done during my entire stay – and trying to recognisably separate it from the grass. Over all this activity brooded an atmosphere of excitement approaching almost paroxysm. I remembered Sister Zoë saying in her overawed tones, 'a grreat man', and how I had then wanted to check this against Jitters's judgment. Seeing that in this climate of expectation I could safely take a break without anyone noticing my absence, I decided to trot over to the presbytery and have a word with him to find out a little more about this eagerly awaited guest of honour, and maybe cadge a cup of authentic coffee. I was just tidying up the clutter of my work table, when Jitters himself appeared.

He jerked his thumb towards the window. 'Himself is coming,' he said darkly; then he gave me a friendly shake of the shoulder, 'mind your manners, Wig. We'll be having His Nibs for supper, unless I'm mistaken.'

He helped himself to a few books, placed them on the desk before me and rolled his eyes ceilingward in a travesty of despair: 'Women!' he whistled significantly, 'What a lot of fuss!'

So after that, and even though the expression 'His Nibs' was a new one to me, there was no need for me to ask his opinion – as I had surmised, this Father Read's appeal was strictly for the less discerning members of the opposite sex. I went back to my work and thought no more about the matter until my attention was interrupted by the noise of a car pulling up on the gravel outside. Something of the nuns' excitement must have infected me unawares though, or else the mere fact of an addition to our limited fauna was in itself an event, for I could not resist going to the window to have a look at – what was it that Hugh had called him? – His Nibs.

The instant I saw him stepping out of the taxi another and better name for him suggested itself (I was using my mnemonic device again, only this time, to do him justice, I must add that the device was quite unnecessary in that he was an unforgettable man): Condor. From his hugely tall and black-enveloped frame, protruded, in fact, an austerely naked head, ringed by a small white collar; and, as if this in itself were not enough, the resemblance to a vulture – albeit to a very clean and glossy one – was reflected too in the gait, the tilt of the head, in the high, hunched shoulders and the flapping of the robe. We later noticed, Martina and I, that the scalp was in reality patched with infinitesimally short grey hairs, and we came to the conclusion that he dramatised a commonplace baldness by shaving – a clever move, really, because the effect was, as I said, unforgettable. I could now begin to see why the nuns had been in such excitement: Father Constantine Read was a truly magnificent specimen of manhood. Vain too, of course – that stuck out a mile – but certainly not without reason, and, as it turned

121

out later, not at all the narrow, church-bound intellect that his book had led me to expect. I discovered that he had written much else besides and only indulged in these breaches of literary taste out of that vanity which was his besetting vice: the fact was that he loved admiration – particularly feminine admiration – and would court it by any means, even down to the publication of coy prayers for cloistered maidens.

I was not introduced to him until dinner at Jitters's that evening, and then I was given the opportunity to appreciate a further and considerable attraction: Condor, in this respect unlike the homonymous bird, had a beautiful voice. This too he administered knowledgeably, counteracting the mellifluous tones by speaking rather lightly and quickly and peppering his utterances with an awkward, husky laugh. I had prepared myself to dislike him, and his striking physical qualities had done but little to predispose me in his favour; instead I found myself increasingly captivated. He was witty and informed and urbane; what is more he had a whimsical, almost mischievous sense of humour and was not only well-versed in philosophy but also well-connected in this field, and famous names in contemporary thought slipped off his tongue with uncontrived simplicity, with reluctance even, as if it were unavoidable but slightly shameful that he, a mere churchman, should admit to possessing such acquaintances. I saw that Jitters too, when actually in his presence and notwithstanding his disparaging comments of the morning, was far from being insensitive to Condor's charm.

We had a pleasant evening; the food was much better than usual, and the Reverend Read, or Constantine, as he straightway insisted on being called – 'Although it hardly seems a fair request to make of anyone – my mother was a fervent convert to Catholicism, you see, and *her* Christian name, need I tell you . . . ' – held forth amusingly and tactfully, bringing both his listeners into the conversation whenever he could (which was admittedly not often), on a meeting of theologians he had recently attended in Amsterdam. I think Hugh was secretly thrilled to hear of the goings on in such exalted clerical circles, and he made several breathless inquiries after members of his own Order whom he thought might have been present. Condor answered carefully and humbly: there had been so many participants and his own circle of acquaintances was so lamentably small and cliquey. He was however on friendly terms with those two sweet fellows . . . and he mentioned a couple of names which made Jitters's eyes expand excitedly.

Martina had not been invited, and in a way this was something of a relief. I found it in fact rather difficult to broach the subject of Martina with Jitters nowadays, let alone be with them together, knowing as I did the nature of the unworthy and ridiculous suspicions which he nourished on her account. It was embarrassing and indeed painful to me – both for him and for her. Now things however had come to the point where I was obliged to bring the matter up with him and to let him know just how sincere and deep my involvement with his she-werewolf had become. Not that I needed his approval – that would be very hard to come by! – nor even his understanding: no, I merely needed his material support. For that afternoon when our love-making had scarcely ended and we were lying there together, joined but spent, on her rickety little iron bed, and drawing strength from the knowledge so well expressed by my favourite English poet that I had found here the true centre of the universe, I had persuaded Martina at last to carry out my experiment and to allow me to spend the night of the oncoming full moon with her: the only condition she stipulated was that I should not be alone. Here, then, was where Jitters came in, for after the scene I had witnessed through the keyhole I could not abide my co-watcher to be Sister Lucy – anyone rather than her, I decided, at the same time aware that 'anyone' was, and could only be, Hugh. If possible we would leave Frogface out altogether. Martina would declare she wanted to go through her psychological crisis this time quite alone; she would ask merely to be locked into her room and left in peace, and Jitters and I would be able to join her later using a second key. Like all the rest, a very simple plan whose only hitch resided once again in the difficulties of persuasion. I had somehow to crack Jitters's resistance.

I went over early to his cottage on the following evening and found him surreptitiously rolling cigarettes to offer to his distinguished guest. He explained that he did not want to have to do the spitting business in front of his suave brother in Christ, and I could see his point very clearly. I told him I quite understood, and apologised for being so early; then I summoned up courage and made my request.

The reaction I got was unforeseeably violent, and I feared for a moment that he was going to have a stroke; tobacco and paper fluttered everywhere and I had to catch him from falling with my arm under his and lower him into one of the unmanageable deckchairs. 'You can't mean it! You can't mean it!' he kept repeating. 'Tell me you don't really mean it, Wig.' Had I not been so worried about eventual repercussions on his already frail state of health, I think that his behaviour would have succeeded in outraging me; as it was, I dashed into the house to look out some brandy or spirits of some kind to steady his nerves. All I could find, however, was some Communion wine and a small bottle of ammonia.

When I got back I gave him a whiff of this on my rolled-up handkerchief and made him take a swig of wine: he had already calmed down somewhat and was now just looking miserable.

'Of course, I knew you were messing around with her,' he said at length when he had got his breath back, 'but you, Wig, *you* – with your brains and your sense and all – falling *in love* with that . . . with that . . . ' He faltered for words, brought a tightly clenched fist to his mouth and bit on it. 'I refuse to believe . . . I refuse. What you suggest is madness. Criminal madness! What? You and I sit there all night, while . . . Go and see for yourself if you don't believe me. Go to the cemetery and see for yourself where the last one finished up!' His protests finished on a shrill bleat, accompanied by a shudder.

More than anger or offence, I was struck by a feeling of insurmountable defeat. I had expected reluctance, a demonstration of fear maybe, but nothing approaching this. As in my dealings with Martina I had again made the mistake of underestimating the gravity of my interlocutor's delusion, and had abruptly reached a point at which I hardly knew any longer what to say or unsay. Until now we had been friends with little or nothing in common; now he seemed to me like the inhabitant of some other world – an absurd, topsy-turvy world peopled with leprechauns, werewolves and what-have-you – with whom there is no authentic possibility of communication, nor ever can be. I was not even upset by the way he had spoken of Martina, for his was a foreign language. Similarly, he too would be deaf to my needs from total lack of understanding. I sat down on the damp grass near his chair and tried to retract, to cheer him up a little, and made him the empty promise that I would do no more of what he called 'brainless meddling', and after a short while he began to recover some shreds of self-possession and to relent: 'Bring her over tomorrow evening, do, by all means, Wig,' he said lamely, aware perhaps at last of having wounded me. 'I'd rather have the pair of you where I can keep an eye on you, if you understand. I've nothing personal against Martina; you do realise that, don't you? Nothing I blame her for, that is. She's not to blame at all. She's only . . . '

'Sssh!' I went softly with a finger to my lips, giving his hand a squeeze as I would to a child in the dark, 'Ssh, Hugh, I understand.'

I think it was at that very moment, or perhaps some minutes later when the tall, gaunt figure of Father Read came striding reassuringly out of the dusk towards us, his face contracted in a shy, welcoming grin, that I knew who to turn to now for help; for here, of course, was the person I had been looking for; here was a wise, sophisticated man of the world, a fellow intellectual who, despite his priestly calling, seemed to have as strong a grip on reality as I did myself. How shortsighted of me to have turned to the other little country bumpkin of a monk when this vastly superior and eminently more suitable helper was at hand.

'Ah! Wine and just the three of us,' he exclaimed gladly, lowering himself gracefully into a deckchair, the folds of his dark robe billowing about him. 'What could be nicer. You wouldn't think there was much work involved in lecturing to a group of charming ladies and hearing a few confessions, but I'm afraid they've quite quinched me today. Taxing job, yours, Hugh. I should think you're relieved to have them taken off your hands for a few days.' He seemed unperturbed by our tenseness and by Hugh's pallor, though he could hardly have failed to notice either, and with faultless manners went on chattering to us about the things which had struck him as amusing during the course of his patiently spent day

126

with the retreating nuns. He managed while maintaining discretion and kindness towards his charges, to be extremely funny about them, and soon had us close to relaxation again. When supper came, he interrupted his comments and covered his mouth like a naughty schoolboy. The lay-sister smiled at him ecstatically and he grinned back, raising his eyebrows and giving her an affectionate look; he seemed indeed to have time and attention for everyone.

'Sister Zoë has been pricking her fingers *on purpose* while she does her embroidery,' he resumed gaily when the nun had withdrawn. 'It started as a penance, but now she has confided in me – outside the confessional, of course, or I wouldn't be sneaking – that she is beginning to *enjoy* it. Now is this a sin, she wonders, and should she desist, or is it the devil trying to ruin her penance, and should she continue? I told her I would have to mull the thing over. I think I'll just tell her she has a prickly problem on her hands and leave it at that!' He beamed at Jitters. 'What do you say, Hugh?'

Jitters grunted, but I could see that – beyond feelings of what was most likely professional jealousy – he was greatly taken by the man. 'I hope you can put in a little work on Sister Lucy,' he suggested timidly. 'After your last visit she was like butter for the best part of a month.'

The conversation drifted comfortably on. It emerged that Frogface was one of the chief figures in Condor's club of admirers. 'She has truly remarkable energy,' he admitted, grimacing slightly to disown the flattery, 'admirable, but to be channelled if possible away from one. Surprisingly good food you get here!'

Jitters and I exchanged a quick glance which he intercepted, and we all laughed: the dramatic atmosphere of earlier had been wholly dissipated.

Jitters left the table early – tired out, I am afraid, by the

127

after-effects of the shock which I had inflicted on him. I regretted this, and felt strong promptings of responsibility as I watched him shuffle off into the house, but I was on the other hand glad to be left alone with Condor so conveniently early, for by the shape and size of the moon I could see that time was running short. Allowing him, therefore, no further urbanities, I launched straight into my story.

At first his round grey eyes expressed nothing more than polite attention, but as I got under way they intensified in roundness, approaching at certain key points (as, for example, when I told him of the velvet bag, and of the bound figure subjected to the reading of the litany) sphericity. He did not interrupt, however, nor indeed make any sound or comment – he just pulled a pipe from somewhere in the spacious black tent of his habit and held it between his teeth, where it remained unlit. In the thickening dusk it was hard to tell what effect my words were having.

I told all I could – leaving out, naturally, any mention of the physical side of my relation to Martina – and tried to impress upon him the urgency and importance of my rescue plan.

'Well, well, well!' he exhaled softly after a considerable silence. 'You're not – no, of course you aren't – pulling an elaborate hoax on me, Ludwig? No, I can tell that you aren't.' He twisted the only available tuft of cranial hair, his eyebrow, meditatively and stared before him into the darkness; then he looked at me sharply again: 'You are not perhaps yourself the victim of such a hoax? I mean,' he hastened to add, 'I mean, you don't think it conceivable that the young Polish lady could be . . . how does one say? . . . having you on? pulling your leg? Dass sie dich auf den Arm nimmt?' Even in this moment of perplexity he could not resist, I noticed, the temptation

128

to parade a snippet of idiomatic German. I returned his gaze severely.

'No, of course not,' he concurred, 'of course not.'

Silence fell; lifted as he said wonderingly, 'Well, well, well!' again a few times over, and then fell again. I hoped that he was using it to do some thinking with that brain of his which had earned him such renown in theological orbits. He must have been; or at least he must have been putting order in his thoughts, for he next spoke to give me a clear and comprehensive summary of all I had told him. The only point he had not fully grasped, he said, was the aberrant nature of Jitters's convictions, so I went over this again. My recapitulation was punctuated by further silence.

'If I have gathered right,' he said finally, 'the only firm believer then in this young woman's sanity is you yourself. You are asking me to be party to a dubious experiment in amateur psycho-therapy, an experiment which is to be conducted behind the backs, so to speak, of those responsible for her, on the strength of an opinion which you have formed – I hope this won't sound too harsh – just as superficially and as rapidly as the psychoanalyst you so much criticize, and which seems to me to be strongly biased by the affection – or to call it by another less *sympathisch* term – attraction which this person awakes in you. I am interested to know how and why I should have occurred to you as likely to second you in such a rash undertaking.'

I remained quite unaffected by the apparent rigidity of this set-piece; I knew that it was only said to test me, and that Condor was every bit as indignant as I was myself over the Convent's treatment of Martina, although for a set of widely different reasons, chief of which was the fact of not having been consulted by the nuns. Stepping up Martina's age to twenty-one – for it seemed a shame

129

to risk weakening my case from fiddling reasons of registration – I returned dispassionately to argue matters from my side: we were very close, I told him, Martina and I (I did not add how close); we understood one another; she was willing to undergo the experiment (I did not pause over how willing, either); she wanted to leave the Convent and lead a normal life as my wife; they had no legal hold over her as she had to my knowledge never been certified as insane; she had received no specific treatment in all the years she had been here; she was talented and clever and was being intellectually isolated. I piled it all on as unemotionally as possible, and must have done it sensibly and well for I could see Condor hooking his head over pensively and really setting a thinking cap on his denuded pate. With a long, beautifully shaped index finger he tapped against his front teeth for a while and then said:

'I am going to surprise you, Ludwig,' ('No, you aren't,' I thought to myself) 'in giving you for the moment – for the moment, mind you – the benefit of a whole deluge of doubts. I think we need say nothing about the matter for the present to the nuns. They have kept me in the dark over this, and I don't think it will hurt therefore for me to do the same, at least while I am making up my mind about which course to follow. I agree with you that they have handled things irresponsibly so far. I must, of course,' and his eyes lit up appreciably, 'have a word with Miss W. herself. Can this be arranged without the nuns suspecting anything, do you think?' I said I felt sure it could be managed somehow: Father Hugh could invite her, or I could just bring her blithely over. I was sure by now that Frogface felt her hold precarious enough to desire avoiding any kind of clash or tension.

'Won't he find that a bit alarming?' asked Condor with a naughty smile. 'Do you think we should suggest a little *garlic* in the menu or something? Oh dear! The confusion that still reigns in the heads of some of our ministers! It is, of course, the great strength of our Church that She is able to sail straight with such a crew aboard – perhaps on Rousseauesque lines the single imperfections cancel each other out – but this now . . . A far cry from the heady atmosphere of Amsterdam! Not that there weren't some pretty unorthodox opinions put forward there too but none – positively none, my dear Ludwig, please believe me – that smacked of naïveté like this.'

I smiled politely and pointed out that garlic was against vampires. 'There you are!' he laughed. 'Confusion again! Crops up all the time!'

'The weak point, though,' he went on, recomposing his face to seriousness, 'and a very weak point if you don't mind my saying so, is your own plan for therapy. It strikes me . . . ', he leant forward and peered at me earnestly through the translucent summer darkness, 'as being a trifle over-crude; but there will be time to tackle this aspect later – after I have seen the . . . the . . . the lady in question.'

In spite of this criticism, which I felt I could anyway convince him later to waive, I was satisfied by the results of our conversation and relieved that at last another rational, cool personality was backing mine. I was glad too to be able to bring things more into the open, and looked forward to showing off the unexpected treasure I had found buried in this musty old Convent to someone capable of appreciating her to the full. Condor shared my feelings: 'I shall be fascinated to meet Miss W. Fascinated. A lady logician and suspected werewolf. What a delightful combination! And what a rare one! This visit is full of surprises – yourself not least, Ludwig. Congratulations on the originality of your choice,' and the grey eyes sparkled at me with a calculated dose of kindly irony.

131

There was a heavy, liver-coloured sunset the following evening. Martina had been granted permission from Frogface – although in fact permission had not been asked – to make a fourth in the all-male supper.

When I went to her room to collect her I noticed that she had made more elaborate preparations in her toilet than usual. The bathroom was strewn with clothes that had been tried on and then discarded, and a film of fresh talcum-powder coated the linoleum. Martina was standing over the basin in a clearing of footprints, nervously snipping at her hair with a pair of nail-scissors.

'Lucy Frog said on no account to let slip that I am a resident here, Ludwig. What do you think of that? Do you suppose she thinks he would interfere if he knew? Is he an interfering sort of man?' Of course, I too had been wondering ever since I had taken Condor into my confidence why he had never been informed about Martina's presence there when surely his moral and intellectual stature, added to the fact that he had for so long acted as confessor and spiritual guide to the community, should have indicated him as a uniquely suitable ally and confidant. I could well understand his own affronted reaction. The answer lay, I felt, in certain facets of Frogface's personality – principally her bossiness and love of organisation but partly too her possessive attitude towards Martina; she evidently felt capable of handling the situation as she had done up till now, with her own roughshod methods, comforted by no more perspicacious support than Jitters's anguished silence, and feeble acquiescence from her direct superior, the Abbess; to have admitted Father Read to the secret would have meant surrendering her conductor's baton and taking a seat among the mere players, albeit the prominent seat, say, of first violin. Yes, I thought grimly to myself, Martina was doubtless her own worst enemy but the

Frog, for all her assurances to the contrary, had been no friend. Well, all things considered, no permanent harm had been done by this, for now the priest had been admitted, but as an ally on *my* side – the side of enlightenment and reason. Could Frogface, I wondered, feel her hold weakening? And how would she react if she could foresee that in a question of days her jealously guarded charge would no longer be needing her, would be discarding the cage of her lycanthropy as she had already that of her agoraphobia, and walking serenely out into a sunny, open world? No more baleful nights of litanies; no more prayers by candlelight. 'My kingdom come, Frog,' I thought to myself with a chuckle of satisfaction. 'My kingdom come, thy kingdom go.'

Martina looked at me questioningly. She was still struggling with her hair which, since I had cut it, had taken to growing fast and slightly horizontal.

'Is he, Ludwig?' she prompted. 'Interfering, I mean?'

I took over the scissors and did a little further pruning around the beloved, anxious little face. I too wanted her to look her best, because Condor for all his vanity and affectation had deeply impressed me and I wanted to make sure of doing likewise, both in my own person and through my connection with Martina. I reassured her: he might be a priest, but he was none the less an exceptionally charming and clever man; she must not let prejudice affect her judgment – not all priests were to be mistrusted by the mere fact of their calling, and not all doctors either. 'And stop fretting so, liebes Herz,' I wound up firmly, planting a kiss on the top of her head, where the parting dissolved into a rebellious, spiky whorl. 'I'm sure you will take to each other very much indeed.' In exchange she gave me a brief, radiant smile only faintly tinged by doubt, and we trotted down the stairs together hand in hand, the rays of the sun glowing

133

on the back of her head with stripey, plum-coloured fury.

In the event it was hard to tell whether she liked him or not, but I was left in no doubt as to the converse. Both priests were there when Martina and I arrived. Jitters gave just a soft flap of the hand in welcome, as I think the pace of events and the presence of his challenging visitor were wearing him down, but Condor rose studiedly to his feet with a great swirl of skirts and took Martina's hand between his own with almost juvenile deference.

'My child, I have heard so much about you,' he began effusively, then sensing from the hurriedly withdrawn hand that this might not be a sufficiently guarded open-ing, he continued smoothly but with less dash, 'I am afraid that my own notions of logic are limited to the sprinkling I was given as a novice,' (I thought this unlikely to be true), 'where we were taught that Aristotle had it all sewn up. Now that, I am told . . . ' and he gave one of his infectious, gauche grins and pulled Martina down in the chair beside his, 'that is a misapprehension. Or, should I say, a lot of nonsense; so I should be very interested to hear from one who knows . . . ' His voice became low and eager and he bent towards her, gripping the arms of the chair with the concentration of a punter listening to the racing results.

I had not failed to notice Martina's initial flush of disquiet at being subjected to such fulsome attention; now she was beginning to answer more freely and detailedly as she got into the stride of her subject, but even so I could tell by the curve of her neck which was slightly arched away from Condor, and by the way she kept scratching rhythmically at her kneecap, that she was suffering from an unprecedented fit of self-consciousness. It hardly surprised me, since the suave Father Read was indeed unleashing a veritable broadside

134

of charm for her benefit, but it hardly pleased me either, and my displeasure became yet more acute during the meal as he continued unashamedly to invest her with the weight of his undivided attention.

She ate little, toying with the food put before her, shifting it from one side of the plate to the other, then building it into heaps and mashing them with her fork – she was normally a keen eater and should have been appreciating the marked improvement in the menu which our visitor's presence had wrought – and it was evident that her unease had not yet subsided. Condor, however, took no notice and battered away gently at her reserve until he had her holding forth, very interestingly too I thought, on the mathematical nebulisation of truth-values. I was sure that the monk's command of the technicalities here was slender, but he managed to conceal this by nodding enthusiastically and by asking half-formed questions and leaving them elegantly suspended until Martina completed them for him; then he would nod again, jerk forward in his chair and say, 'Precisely, *precisely*. That was just the point that was bothering me.' Oh yes, he was clever and no mistake. Admirably clever and admirably charming. Martina was getting too carried away to notice the artifice, though, or to notice my misgivings and poor Jitters's boredom. Out of respect for our nominal host, therefore, and perceiving that besides tedium and exclusion he was beginning to experience tiredness as well, I made one or two attempts at breaking up the conversation. When these failed I used more drastic measures and challenged Condor point-blank to a game of chess, so loudly and energetically that he could hardly refuse me. Hugh took advantage of the interruption and with another weak salute sidled quietly off to bed, while Martina stayed on beside us, sitting rather closer to the monk than to me and poring over the board discussing moves with him, so that I was obliged to observe the spectacle which had so disconcerted me during supper of their two heads – the furry red one and the cold, bare, grey one – bent together in engrossed debate. At least, Martina was engrossed; whereas the suspicion came to me and stayed with me that what Condor was doing was not concentrating on the game but flirting. To be sure, it was a very cerebral and very polished way of doing so, but it was flirting all the same. I wondered crossly how Martina could fail to notice this and how she could fail to be as disconcerted as myself; then reflected more comfortingly that perhaps she had indeed noticed, and had been self-conscious and put off her food on that account. Anyway, I was more than relieved to see her get to her feet and bid us both good-night, the more so as I was getting into a tricky position with my queen and did not like the thought of her witnessing even a temporary setback, let alone defeat, at the hands of this particular adversary.

I smiled up at her in approval; such a wide smile in fact that I was unable to erase it when my opponent offered glibly to accompany her back to the house, and I was left staring after their departing shadows with it still stuck inanely across my face, too set upon rescuing my queen to leave the game and follow them, too distracted by their togetherness to concentrate on my move; the discomfort of my position aggravated by the fact that the longer Condor was absent the more time I had for strategy and the less able I was to make use of it.

Enervated by the very neatness of the dilemma I pushed my chair away from the board and tried instead to assess my feelings. I was not – no, I was sure I was not – straightforwardly jealous of the monk: that would have been an unworthy emotion and easy to deal with. No, my feelings were more complicated. I trusted instinctively the man's intellectual competence – indeed not only instinctively, for I had had both opportunity and ability to judge it. I had moreover personally requested his intervention, had observed and accounted for his vanity, and had wanted him to be impressed by Martina. What then could be more natural than that his interest in the case should involve independent investigation and a little innocuous, sublimated flirting? If this did not surprise me, why should it bother me so? Was I bothered by the priest or by the man? Did I fear Martina would like him too little (to little to allow him to participate in the experiment, or to allow it to succeed?) or too much (too much to what?); or that she would like the priest too little and the man too much? Or the other way around? Or was I simply regretting that I had turned to anyone for help other than myself?

These and other queries spun round elusively in my head, as fleet and many-sided as waltzers, coming to a halt unanswered only when I saw Constantine re-emerge at last, dark and undulating, from the paler shadow of the trees.

I made a rapid, conventional move to save if not queen at least face, hoping it would not seem I had been devoting a lot of thought to the matter, and we resumed play in silence, Condor swooping down on the board single-mindedly and without any apology for his delay. His single-mindedness may have been merely a pose, however, for he now began playing a much less adroit game: I beat him easily in the end, and between moves had the leisure to reflect further on the intricate form of intellectual jealousy – if this was what it was – I felt towards him, and which was in no way assuaged by the present minor victory.

With a flick of his long spare forefinger he toppled his king and watched it roll gently to immobility. 'Sah mat:

137

the King is dead,' he said with a pleasant and seemingly contented smile. 'I'm afraid I didn't give you much of a game. But then I suppose it is hard for you to find anyone who does? Perhaps at University?' He must have understood, though, that this was not time for small or even medium-sized talk, for instead of waiting for an answer he added immediately and in a much more kindly tone, 'You are wanting to know what I think of your fiancée, of course.'

I nodded. He rose tactfully and switched off the light bulb which Jitters had rigged up for our convenience.

'There, that's better. Now, what do I think of your Martina? What do I think? Well, Ludwig, let me not beat about the bush but say straight out that I think she is remarkable to the point of freakishness. A remarkable brain, remarkably housed, carrying within it a remarkable history, and tainted by a remarkable discrepancy. Epithets do not usually dry up on me in this way,' he scratched at the invisible stubble on his scalp, 'so there's proof for you of how profoundly she has moved me. I quite understand – quite, quite understand now – your position and your desire . . . ' He paused a second and somewhat unfortunately over his wording, 'to rescue her from whatever her predicament may be. I am still, though, a little perplexed over the way you want to set about it – more perplexed, in fact, now that I have seen her.'

'You think we ought to call in professional help from outside? A qualified analyst, or someone like that?'

'No, nothing of the kind,' he said, a trifle sharply. 'That was not at all what I meant.'

I waited for more, half-wishing he had left the light on since all I could see now were varying depths of darkness – the nearer the darker – culminating in the pitch-black figure at my side; and as the voice resumed the need for illumination made itself felt more strongly still. For believe it or not, my chosen helper, my rational aide-de-camp who was to flank me in my private battle against the forces of superstition had launched into a disquisition not on techniques of psychotherapy as I had been expecting, but on – of all things – sinfulness. He was actually talking, and in all seriousness, about sin. About evil.

I peered through the darkness, my eyes now growing gradually more accustomed to it, at the grey globe of his head, trying to gain comprehension. What was he up to? Where was he leading? Could I be hearing him aright, I wondered dazedly, doing my best to grasp the sense of his words. What had happened to effect such a bewildering change of outlook?

'There are *levels* of description,' his carefully reared voice was saying – although this is only a very approximate rendering for I was too taken aback to register anything other than the gist – 'a human action, my dear Ludwig, can be described at microbiological level as the interaction of so many cells; or again, at a slightly higher level, as the mechanical functioning of a single organism.' He raised his hand to shoulder height to indicate growth. 'Higher still would be the description in terms of purposeful behaviour on behalf of the single organism, then of its teleological behaviour, and this again within the context of a social organism such as a family, a state, and so forth. To see and describe it in terms of good and evil is none other than to reach the highest level,' his hand which had been slowly ascending now soared into the air, its sleeve flapping wildly; 'the highest of which we are capable, that is; the highest intelligible to us.'

So here at last, I realised vexedly, was the priest speaking. It came as something of a let-down after the picture I had built of him, but I can hardly say that I was

139

surprised. Disappointed, but not surprised. He was keeping, mind you, to a high level of abstraction, but I felt sure that sooner or later he would descend to the concretion of Martina's case. How he would achieve this – how he would manage to tie moral considerations into what was after all a perfectly plain matter of slight (well, to be honest, not so slight) psychological derangement – was something I ought of course to have waited to hear; but I found myself instead in the grip of an emotion close to embarrassment or intolerance but stronger than either and which annulled any patience or sympathy that I might, indeed should, have felt for my interlocutor's argument. I did not want to see where he was leading, sensing prematurely that it was a destination that would diminish him in my eyes: would perhaps, and more importantly, render him unsuitable for the supporting role of spectator-cum-witness which I had assigned him. I wanted things done my way or not at all; I had no need or time for an airing of his irrelevant opinions. After the demonstration of elegantly cerebral court he had paid Martina that evening, to say nothing of his making off with her like that into the night for the best part of half an hour, I did not even like him very much any more; and the expression of friendly, perplexed concern which his voice now conveyed seemed to me no longer to indicate availability but the desire to meddle, to interfere and to distort.

I cannot remember what words I used, nor how careful I was or more likely wasn't in declining to listen further to what he was on about. I fear I may have been more than a little abrupt. I do remember though that I managed to stop the flow of unwelcome words in the end by pinning him down to an *'aut, aut'* decision: if he agreed to help me on my terms well and good, I stated flatly, if not then I would be obliged to handle the matter at a very different level. And at that point I think I mentioned a whole list of authorities to whom I would turn in order to obtain Martina's release: lawyers, psychiatrists, the police. I may even have intimated I would contact the press. All empty threats, of course, for I would never have exposed her in such a cruel way, but Condor seemed convinced by my show of determination for he rolled back his sleeves in absolute silence, rather like a surgeon preparing for an operation, and neared his face to mine with a long, troubled look.

'If that is your last word on the matter, Ludwig,' he said quietly, 'as indeed you have gone to great lengths to convince me that it is; and if the complexities of the situation seem to you to be gratuitously put there like so many obstacles between you and the carrying out of your truly "crucial" experiment, fit for nothing but to be swept aside as fast as possible, then by all means let us go ahead as you wish.'

'You will help me then in the original plan?' I urged, needing to obtain explicit confirmation.

'Which night will it be, exactly?' he inquired cautiously, rubbing his fingers backwards and forwards over the pinpricks of silvery stubble which were now faintly visible and glinting in the moonlight.

I had worked out the dates carefully. 'Not tomorrow but the next night,' I said in a dry, businesslike way. 'I think the best thing would be for us to meet in my room first and then go on together to Martina's turret, where she will be waiting for us. She will be locked in, of course, at her own request, but I have already managed to obtain a duplicate key, so it will all be very simple.'

Condor made no answer. 'I advise you to bring a book,' I added less brusquely, trying to soften the tension between us. 'I think we'll be in for a long and uneventful vigil.'

Without breaking his silence he rose, switched on the light again and gave me a weak but not unfriendly smile. All things considered, he had taken my overbearing tactics rather well: he did not seem at all put out or offended – only a trace more distant perhaps than formerly.

'I can count on your being there, then?' I insisted.

At this he gave a little twitch of annoyance, and pressing his fingertips to the hollow of his eyes said in a tired but firm voice, 'Most certainly, Ludwig. I will be with you well before midnight. Don't . . . ' He paused for a moment and granted me a close, frontal stare which more than any words assured me of his sincerity. 'Don't go without me, will you? On no account.'

'I'll wait,' I said.

He gave me another searching look and then lowered his heavy, grey lids. 'Perhaps it would not be a bad idea if I had just one little further chat with Martina tomorrow . . . ?'

But beyond a shrug I made no reply to that one. There was, I reckoned, nothing I could do to stop him seeing her if he wanted to, and I felt it impolitic to lay down any more conditions when I had already obtained so much. Let him go ahead. Let him talk to her. Martina was so wholly mine by now that whatever he might say, however much he might drone on to her about sin and redemption and what have you, he could exercise – of this I was fundamentally sure – no more influence over her than he could over myself.

6

In my writings over the years I have made frequent and heavy use of what is called the 'negative counterfactual'; for particularly when dealing with the slippery notion of cause it is often useful and sometimes indispensable to be able to open up a kind of bracket in your reasoning and muse on the implications of an event not taking place. Before entering the final and most dramatic phases of my reminiscences – although not, strange to say, the most painful to recall since things happened in such rapid succession and plunged so steeply to degeneration that even in retrospect there was hardly space for anything but stupor – I could not forgo the fruitless temptation to make a little further use of this melancholy device.

If x had not happened, I asked myself sadly, what then? If I had not acted as I did; if I could go back and negate at least one of the antecedent conditions, what difference would this have made? What might have happened? More poignantly still, what might not have happened? And which factor should I have amended? Which, if any, had been directly responsible? Was it my deafness to all other needs except my own? My blinkered cocksureness? My inexperience? My incapacity to appreciate any shading, any realm of indeterminacy

143

between a Manichean polarity of black and white, true and false, existent and non-existent? Should I have borne with Condor that evening, listened to what he was trying to tell me? And would this perhaps have given me an insight into what he was preparing to do? If I had been a little more patient, a little more perceptive, should I not have been able to foresee that he had no intention of adhering to my plan but was already formulating an alternative one of his own – that my simple, empirical experiment was not only incomprehensible, but repugnant to him?

Or if, the next day, instead of watching from my window the far-off figures of Martina and Constantine as they wandered across the Convent lawns deep in talk (again the unacceptable picture of their proximity came before me, and I could see with harsh misgiving the two incompatible heads – the gaunt, grey one bent down towards the fiery blob of Martina's – their two contrasting forms: how on earth, I asked myself angrily, could they find so much to say to one another?); if instead of watching them from afar, feeling excluded, bewildered, and then closing myself off in an offended silence, I had had the humility to speak to Martina afterwards? If, instead of feigning indifference, I had made her tell me what had been said, would that not have given me some clue of what was going on in Condor's mind? Or in her mind too, for that matter? Surely Condor's ascendancy over her could not have been so immediate? Surely there was a moment, if only I had recognised and grasped it, at which I still could have intervened and made her listen? Was my plan wrong? Would it have worked? Why didn't they listen to me? Why didn't they let me try? Why did they – and in particular I mean why did Martina – opt instead for such a different solution? Could there have been a happier ending?

Conjecture like curiosity is rarely idle, but in this case it proved so – if one can discount, that is, the suffering it caused me. Whether my plan, if it had been given a chance, would have worked, or what changes its success might have brought about in my life were reflections best left in the limbo of unformulated hypotheses where they belonged, I admitted defeatedly, as I shifted my position in the hot, rumpled bed of the Convent's guest-room. The mattress was new and springy and symmetrically dotted with small, hard buttons; and as I twisted my body to try and avoid at least some of them I could not help wondering for a moment what had become of the one I used to sleep on – the one on which the signs of my desire for Martina had been etched as on a map; the one I had sighed into, tossed on sleeplessly for nights, dreamed on and on later occasions loved on, talked on, laughed on, planned on and dreamed on again and again. Thrown away, most likely. Burnt. Destroyed.

More idle conjecture. I was nearly through now, though. My watch by the bedside marked nearly three o'clock. I hoped I would manage to get it over with quickly and snatch a little sleep at least before dawn.

Things went, of course, not as they had to, for there was plenty of leeway for them to go otherwise, but as they did. An inflexible truism. Besides which, they also went very fast. On that, our second to last evening, Martina ate in her room. I called in to see her before going over to Jitters and found Frogface sitting there with a smug look on her face, laying out a wall of dominoes. 'Martina has the beginnings of a cold this evening, haven't you, Martina?' she said complacently. 'So I am keeping her company for a bit. Early bed all round would be a good idea, don't you think?'

I raised my eyebrows in query at Martina, who was

sitting upright on the very edge of the bed, already in her dressing-gown. She nodded at me and gave me a wide, confident smile. I had not spoken to her since her chat with Condor, and was still greatly put out by the sheer length of time that they had spent together, but when she smiled I felt instantly reassured for it was the loving, trusting smile I knew so well, speaking the sort of lazy, tacit intimacy that followed our love-making. It told me clearer than words that nothing had changed between us; that she was still with me.

'See you tomorrow, Ludwig,' she said softly.

'If your cold is better,' put in Frog sharply, intercepting our looks with the inquisitive pink beam of her glasses, 'otherwise I think you had better stay in bed.'

I ignored her – little did she realise, I thought with a warm foretaste of triumph, that tomorrow was the day she was to be ousted from her post of custodian for good and all – smiled lovingly back at Martina, and went over to the presbytery for supper.

I had hoped that Jitters would retire early himself and leave me the opportunity for a final re-examination of strategy with Constantine – a kind of dress-rehearsal, as it were, before the actual night – but when I reached the cottage I noted with displeasure that no such opportunity would now crop up: there was a fourth guest, and evidently a very important one. I had in fact noticed on my way over a large, metal-grey Wolseley parked discreetly some distance down the main drive, but I had not given the matter much thought; now I realised its significance. An elegantly clad cleric, wearing a dark cassock with a thin piping of purple round its edges and a startlingly large silver cross and chain, was sitting, glass in hand, in one of the chairs. Thinking back, I can of course see a further significance that escaped me at the time: this Bishop, or Monsignore, or whatever he was, had evidently been sent for by Constantine himself – for I do not think that either Frogface or Jitters played much part in all this, at least not at this stage – to help him with the rival plan he was cooking up behind my back. The approval of some high-ranking ecclesiastical authority must in fact have been a formal prerequisite to the very enactment of his scheme.

Nothing of this occurred to me though that evening. What did occur to me, and compellingly, was simply that I was outnumbered; that there were three priests and then myself. Three priests against myself. And as I walked towards them a silly little rhyme from infancy came into my head, a jingle that our Tyrolean nurse used to sing to us about three owls on a chest; for they reminded me of a trio of owls as they sat there on their precarious perches, blinking and chattering together in the twilight. Or, better still, if I may be forgiven yet another ornithological metaphor, they reminded me of a trio of birds but three very different ones: a vulture, a sparrow and a guinea-fowl.

It is unforgivable of me that I did not sense that something was up – that their specificity was forged by some closer bond than just their mutual priesthood; but no suspicion of the kind entered my head. I felt, as I said, merely irritated at the presence of a stranger thwarting my intent to be alone with Condor, and uncomfortably over-priested.

Dinner – for this was no supper but a three-course meal carried, not wheeled, by a string of awed lay-sisters who waited on us throughout the meal observing strict criteria of precedence – passed tolerably easily. Condor slid gracefully to my aid a couple of times, setting the Monsignore right about my nationality, which even after this correction he took steadfastly to be German, and age, which with similar constancy and quite unaffected by the thickness of my beard he seemed to estimate at roughly sixteen or so, referring to me kindly but unyieldingly as 'this young laddie here', unwilling perhaps to have to recognise in me otherwise a recent enemy.

I became increasingly restless. Communication with Martina had undergone a set-back, partly on account of my stupid pride and partly on account of her own ridiculous habit of shutting herself away during the critical days of her imaginary metamorphosis; and now Constantine too was out of reach. Yet there were so many details that still needed going into, so many things that needed saying. I fervently hoped that an occasion might arise after dinner, but it became clear to me that we – or rather they, for I am afraid that I excused myself and left as soon as I decently could – were in for a long evening when Monsignore confessed to me, rubbing his hands together in joyful anticipation, that he was a slave to the same passion as Father Hugh and had come over with the express intention of indulging in it with him. I nodded wordlessly and then watched in puzzlement as Condor and he came back from the car carrying two large wooden boxes, half-expecting them to be crates of beer, for Jitters to my knowledge had evinced no other passion, but recognising instead with scarcely abated puzzlement a large, wind-up gramophone and a case of records. The mutual passion, it transpired, was that of listening to opera. I didn't give sufficient thought to this either at the time, preoccupied as I was by the prospect of the next decisive evening, but if only I had, this fact in itself would have been enough to have set me on my guard, seeing that in our many conversations Jitters had never let on to me about his penchant for music but had on the contrary often spoken rather mockingly about mine. How very blind I was over the whole affair: how very blind and how very foolish. As I took my leave and threaded my way through the beeches by the light of a menacingly round moon the opera session was already in progress; and I can remember hearing the brittle, piercing soprano of Amelita Galli-Curci, made brittler still by Monsignore's prototypical gramophone, chirping with a peal of operatic laughter the opening bars of Verdi's aria, 'Sempre libera degg'io folleggiare.' Sempre libera: ever free. Poor tragic Martina. Poor Condor. Poor anyone whose path crossed hers. I have never wanted to listen to *Traviata* since.

Next day I did not get a chance of seeing Martina, who, obedient to Frogface's strictures, remained closeted in her bedroom, but I managed to have a moment's conversation with her through the keyhole before lunch.

'All set then for tonight?' I whispered.

'Yes, yes,' she answered hurriedly, 'I do really have a cold, you know, Ludwig.'

'You're not frightened?' I asked. 'Not nervous?' Her voice sounded miserable.

'With you I will never be frightened, Ludwig,' she said solemnly.

'Father Read told you that he is going to be there too? Does that worry you?'

'Yes, I know. He told me. It makes no difference – anyone will do.'

'What else did he say?' I asked leadingly, hoping for a fuller account.

'Oh, nothing in particular. Just the usual old priest stuff. The importance of prayer and all that.'

'He took a long time over it,' I said dubiously. 'He's not backing out or anything?'

There was a moment's silence.

'I don't think he thinks much of your plan, Ludwig,' she said carefully, 'but I'm sure he won't let us down at the last moment. I'm sure he'll come, I mean. He said he might be a bit late though, but not to worry. He's away for the day today, you see, but he promised he would be back in time.'

'He mentioned nothing to me about being away,' I said crossly. Now there was indeed no possibility of giving him any last-minute instructions, and I began to feel as if he had already partially betrayed me.

'Oh, Ludwig, don't be silly. It doesn't matter what time it is; what time we choose to do it, I mean,' said Martina. 'I was just starting to take a sensible view of things, thanks to you, and now it's you who are being the superstitious one. What difference does it make if it is midnight, or eleven, or even one for that matter? It's only a question of getting me over this ridiculous hump, isn't it? You said so yourself, Ludwig, didn't you, that it's all in my mind? Father Read can hold my hands, and you can take off the mask, and then I can look at myself in the mirror; and then it will all be over. It's as easy as that, isn't it, Ludwig? That's all we have to do, isn't it?' By the sound of her voice you would have thought that she was thoroughly bored by the whole thing.

'Of course it is, Liebling,' I whispered back coaxingly through the keyhole. I was glad she was being so commonsensical about it at last, but all the same I didn't want her to remain alone too long that evening for fear she work herself up into a state of nerves, making the smooth carrying out of the experiment more difficult. 'I've got the key, anyway,' I told her. 'If he's late coming back, then I will come on my own, and sit here and keep you company until he shows up.'

'Oh, don't do that!' came Martina's voice in a horrified whisper. 'Oh, please not, Ludwig. Wait for Father Read, however late he is. I know he will come. He said he would. Wait until he comes, I beg of you!' This was a more recognisable version of Martina, and one which overwhelmed me with tenderness.

'I won't do anything you don't completely want,' I promised. 'Get some sleep this afternoon; read a book; do the crossword; whatever you like, but keep calm, and don't worry. When this is all over we shall be leaving here together, remember. We will be starting our new and perfectly ordinary life – Herr and Frau Doktor, off to London together to set up house.'

She made no reply, but a gentle laugh came from behind the door. I went downstairs to lunch with appetite, feeling reasonably satisfied with what I had accomplished: not that we were safely in port yet, for there was still the last and steepest obstacle to overcome, but just by keeping my head – by using it too, undeniably but principally just by keeping it – I had already gained quite a victory over the forces of unreason. This is what I thought.

In reality these forces were anything but vanquished – they were merely quiet because preparing a terrible comeback, and Martina was already enlisted on their side; indeed I sometimes think that she was at their very head. Anyway, she duped me well into waiting for Condor, and by the time I went into action without him it was of course far too late.

It was in fact not until a quarter to midnight that I finally made up my mind, and left the window where I had been sitting tensely for well over two hours listening in vain for the sound of his returning car. The moon – already a prominent enough feature – was overplaying its part, shining with metallic clarity on the hushed garden and deserted drive; but from Martina's turret came the customary weak flicker, creating a timid variation in the lighting scheme of otherwise monochrome silver and telling me that she was there, awake and waiting.

151

It was high time I went to her, I decided, for what if Constantine never came? What if he had ratted on us, or was genuinely unable to make it? That would mean waiting another full month, and my engagement as librarian expired before then. No, whatever I had promised it was no good waiting further; this was a time for quick decisions and quicker action; Martina needed me and I must go to her. I laced my gymshoes tightly, murmuring invectives at the monk's unreliability, pocketed the key to Martina's room and closed the door quietly behind me.

The corridor was empty and still and I paced it almost at a run, avoiding the creaky floorboards with ease and agility – I could have done so blindfold, so familiar was I by now with their layout – until I reached the door to Martina's bathroom. The handle turned smoothly but to my surprise the door remained fast, and it was not until I had shoved at it impatiently for the fourth or fifth time that the possibility of her having locked herself in occurred to me. When it did – when I was forced to admit that push or rattle as I might there was no question of the lock yielding – it was immediately replaced by other and more disturbing possibilities: perhaps the door had been locked not by Martina herself but by Frogface; perhaps she had not relinquished her status of monthly gaoler so easily; perhaps indeed she was still inside there with Martina, carrying out the same ritual watch as before; perhaps it had been impossible for Martina to be rid of her. What matter then, I thought to myself defiantly, this merely meant that the third party would have to be Frogface after all, not Condor, and surely it didn't make much odds either way at this juncture.

I began shaking the door quite noisily, knocking and calling out Martina's name, but no sound came from beyond. Seriously alarmed, I tried next to force the door

152

with my shoulder, then, remembering the rudimentary character of most inside locks, I desisted and traced my way instead back along the corridor, collecting as I went as many keys as I was able to find from the adjacent rooms. Opening one of the doors I was struck by a strong scent of tobacco and I switched on the light to confirm my suspicions. Yes, this was the guest-room allotted to the nuns' confessor: it was empty, but showed signs of very recent occupation. There was a tray beside the bed with the remains of the same meal which had been dished out to Jitters and myself that very evening; the bed was crumpled, the ashtray dirty. It looked as if Condor had been shamming his visit to London and had remained hidden in his room all evening. Now why, I asked myself bewilderedly, should he have done a thing like that? And the nuns party to the trick. What was going on?

My alarm began to verge on panic. I slammed the door to, paying no heed now to the noise I might be making, and raced back to the turret.

The second key I tried turned in the lock with a bit of effort; the door gave way before me and I charged through the bathroom, calling Martina's name as I went and fumbling in my pocket for the key to the turret it-self.

I had reckoned on finding Martina in the clutches of Frogface or Condor, or possibly both, never imagining that I would find no one there at all. Yet when I burst into the room, that was how I found it: empty – empty and strangely tidy. The night-light had been left burning on the table, but all Martina's books were neatly closed and stacked, her dressing-gown was laid out at the foot of the bed and two small, downtrodden slippers were ranged side by side on the mat below it. It certainly didn't look as if she had been dragged off anywhere against her will; it looked, quite to the contrary, as if she had carefully made all the necessary preparations, deliberately left the light on so that it would seem she was still there, and had then quitted the room of her own accord, locking both doors behind her. Both doors? Of course. The second door had been locked in order to delay my arrival – in order to gain time. The light had been left burning in order to allay my suspicions and to gain time. I had been made to wait for Condor's phantom return in order to gain time. But time for what? Why had she done all this? Why the lies? Furthermore, had she left alone? Where had she gone to? Where was she now? And where was Condor?

Condor. Condor. The name rang in my head with a grim, leaden sound, silencing all the questions and making things suddenly clear to me: for it was so simple – I had been tricked into waiting in vain like this all evening so that he could sabotage my experiment and go ahead with some rival plan of his own. But what plan?

I sat down heavily on the bed – the erstwhile centre of my happy universe – and gripped the iron rungs in a new and unwelcome condition of impotence: every second that passed was yet more time wasted and more time for whatever scheme he was up to. What was he doing to Martina? Where, where could they be? How could I set about finding them? I could hardly search every room in the house – it would take far too long; besides which, they might be somewhere in the inaccessible regions of the enclosure, or he might have taken her clean away.

On top of my misery and indecision I began now to feel the promptings of that amalgam of jealousy and resentment which I had suffered from on the evening I had introduced Martina to Condor. From their first moment of meeting I had seen, in fact, that there was a strong – an uncannily strong – bond of sympathy between them. I had felt it instantly, and resented it just as soon. Could it

154

not be that even now they were prowling round the grounds together in the moonlight; could it not be that he was holding her hand in his in a tender, fatherly grasp and trying to cure her of her absurd beliefs by showing her their incompatibility with another set of beliefs – his own – less raw, maybe, but equally far-fetched, equally absurd? Was it not, I asked myself bitterly, that from the very start and despite the intimacy of our physical relationship she had been closer to Condor than ever she had been to me? Condor and redcap – the birds of my classification; birds of a feather, creatures of the air, free to flit in regions where my solid, earthbound intellect for all its power could never follow them? Where were they now, the two of them? What were they up to together and who could I turn to to find out?

I sat up with a start, recognising at last amid the jumble of queries which had been buzzing around chaotically in my head one to which there was a simple answer: before doing something irrevocably rash like bursting into the nuns' quarters at this hour of night demanding an explanation of Martina's whereabouts, I must of course make a prior attempt at pumping Jitters. Come to think of it he had been more than usually on edge that evening, so more likely than not he had a good inkling of what was being architected behind my back and with a bit of pressure I would get it out of him.

Having decided this I lost no more time, but padded stealthily and fast down the stairs and out into the garden, towards the pale, squat outline of the priest's cottage. Consulting my watch by the bright light of the moon I could see that it was already three minutes after midnight – my indecision and all the fiddling about with locks and keys had cost me over a quarter of an hour.

There was no light from the cottage, but when I knocked at the window of Jitters's bedroom he opened it almost immediately and I saw that he was fully dressed and wide awake, almost as if he had been expecting a visit.

'Good Lord, it's you, Ludwig!' he said nervously, looking very taken aback and peering anxiously out into the shadows behind me. 'What are you doing out there? Are you alone?'

I had had no time to decide on the form my pumping was to take. 'Where's Martina?' I asked angrily, the urgency in my voice making it sound more of a yelp than a question. 'And where's Constantine? You'd better tell me if you know. Their rooms are empty. He's taken her off somewhere, I'll bet. I'll wake the whole Convent if you don't tell me right now where they are!'

· 'Hush now, Ludwig,' he whispered at me unhappily. 'Don't shout so. Martina is quite safe. Father Read is having another little chat with her, that's all.'

'A little chat!' I spat at him in fury. 'A little chat! Is that so? The two of them together at this time of night, on the night of the full moon – a girl who thinks she's a werewolf and priest who thinks he's God incarnate – and all you can tell me is that they are having a little *chat*?'

Anger invaded me wholly, and in its throes I think I must have taken bodily hold of him, for I saw him wince and try unsuccessfully to draw back from the window.

'Where, for God's sake, where are they?' I shouted, receiving no reply beyond a dumbfounded, round-eyed stare. 'Where? Where? Where?' I went on shouting with a childish obstinacy, convinced that it was just a question of repeating the question often and loud enough. And as I shouted I saw his head bob back and forth in time to my words and felt the pliant rim of his dog-collar twist in my grip – he was giving in.

'Ludwig! Wiggie!' he pleaded at last, choking for breath. 'This isn't like you at all. Keep quiet for a moment, will you, and I'll explain. There's nothing to get worked up about.'

I released my hold and watched him draw back from me in blatant relief. He must have interpreted my pumping efforts as bona fide intent to throttle him, for as he spoke he kept fingering his crumpled collar with wonderment and giving a spate of offended coughs. 'You must try and understand,' he said nervously, his manner half-way between apologetic and patronising. 'Come on inside like the sensible fellow you are, and I'll try and explain.'

In spite of my impatience I followed tamely in the end. It was relief enough to know that he could at least give me the information I wanted; although, looking back on it, it meant more precious time wasted. No, not precious any more really, for by then I don't think time would have made much difference. I reckon that Condor stuck by the convention of the witching-hour of midnight, so it was presumably all over by then anyway.

What Jitters told me, crouched miserably over his chess table and cradling the pieces in his hands to mask his trembling, was that it had been decided on the evening before – having obtained of course, he added, her full consent and an *ad hoc* authorisation from the appropriate authority (hence the music-loving Monsignore, I realised belatedly, cursing my shortsightedness) – to exorcise Martina.

'It's an unusual proceeding, I know,' he went on haltingly, fumbling with the chess pieces and watching me with apprehension. 'It's not what I would have chosen myself. Not something to be rushed into like this, but Father Constantine was so insistent. He seemed to think that if he didn't take action, then you, Ludwig, would go ahead with your crazy scheme, and that would have been . . . Because yours *was* a crazy scheme, you

157

know . . . ' He trickled to a stop and looked at me ruefully, cringing defensively behind the chess board as I rose to my feet once more.

'You mean to say,' I began incredulously, 'you mean to say that that monk has inveigled Martina into accepting . . .' but I found myself unable to continue, so profound was my disgust of the word 'exorcism' and all it connoted. It was then as I had feared – no, worse than I had feared: the dreaded vulture had taken Martina off somewhere to practise on her a revolting, primitive ritual; the black, evil bird of ill-omen had taken my little love away and was holding her in his power at that very moment, subjecting her in all probability to some humiliating torture devised by his Church in the darkest ages and never altered since. I tried to imagine what the ritual could consist in: was the poor, bedevilled victim tied to a plank, and then gagged and purged? Or did the exorcist just utter a few curses and then wait patiently for a spontaneous departure of the devils? Where did the bells and books and candles come in? Was it all done verbally nowadays, or did the priest still enter into bodily struggle with the enemy's forces?

At the thought of this last possibility a second curtain of anger rang down again on the conscious part of my mind and I watched with a certain detached interest the chess pieces fly in all directions as I lurched towards Jitters, aiming for his collar once more.

'They're in the church, Wiggie,' he said in an almost soundless whisper, dodging sideways to avoid my thrust. 'Don't go . . .' But I was past him and out of the house before he could finish his warning. I sensed, though, that he was following me as I ran at full tilt towards the church, and heard in confirmation the faint puff of his breath and the clip-clop of his sandals on the flagstones behind me. The distance was negligible, yet it

158

seemed as in the tritest of dreams to take me an unaccountably long time to cover. Once there, I came up
against further frustration, since this door too was bolted
from the inside.

With the same unthinking drive of earlier when the
bathroom door had stood between myself and my objective, I began rattling at the lock and then hurling myself
at the door itself, but was prevented from this by Jitters,
who had now caught up with me and had splayed himself theatrically across the entrance, arms outstretched.

'Stop that, Wig!' he ordered firmly, his fear abating
now that he was no longer the direct object of my rage.
'You'll only hurt yourself. There's another door at the
back.'

I ran breathlessly to the rear of the building still closely
tailed by Jitters, and tried this door too with the same
mindless energy and negative result.

'I'll give you a leg up,' said Jitters, strangely calm and
helpful of a sudden like one humouring a maniac, which
was I suppose in a sense the case; 'then you can have a
look through the window and see if everything's all
right. Keep calm though, she'll be all right with Constantine – she's in safe keeping.'

I put my foot on the stirrup his frail invalid's hands had
improvised, but it gave beneath my weight almost immediately and I slipped, face and hands badly rasped by
thorns, down to the ground once more without having
caught even the briefest glimpse of the inside.

'Chairs,' said Jitters promptly, 'one on top of the
other,' and I found myself running back along the path to
the presbytery in tacit obedience to his suggestion.

The deckchairs were of course useless for the purpose I
had in mind and I began rapidly scanning the other items
of furniture, looking for something solid and high
enough to enable me to reach the window. The only

thing that seemed suitable was a high, narrow bookcase where Jitters's own collection of detective novels and prayer books were housed. Aware of nothing but the passing of time and still more time and grudging every second of it, I started to clear the shelves of their contents, sweeping each row impatiently on to the floor in a cloud of dust, only to find that I then had to shift them further off in order to obtain enough space in which to lever the bookcase on to my shoulders: now that I really needed him, Jitters was no longer there.

At last, sweating and fumbling, I managed to heave the bookcase into the air and to balance it on my back in a makeshift position, where it weighed on me heavily, the breasts of a caryatid biting into my backbone.

Wielding it thus tremulously aloft I blundered out of the house, the corners crashing into other pieces of furniture and thumping against the walls, and started hobbling crabwise down the path towards the church.

Then, as soon as I was able, I swung round frontways and instantaneously let drop my burden, which fell with a crash behind me; for while I had been engaged in my furniture-hunt things had been happening. The door of the church was wide open; light was pouring from both door and windows, and I could just discern the silhouette of a nun running at full tilt towards the main building, her robes hitched up round the waist in a grotesque fashion. Bad things had been happening: I could smell disaster, even from a distance.

When I reached the church Jitters was once more splayed melodramatically across the threshold barring my way, but this time there was nothing melodramatic about his expression, which was one of unmitigated and palpably unfeigned horror.

'For God's sake, keep away!' he shouted at me hoarsely. 'Don't, Wig, don't go in there . . .'

I brushed past him as easily as if he had been a cobweb. I had not allowed myself to imagine what I would find inside the church, but I must none the less have already mentally adjusted myself to the catastrophic dimension for I felt nothing beyond a sort of flat resignation. Something terrible had happened to Martina, of that I was certain, but it was something that carried with it a taste of finality, and it no longer seemed so urgent to discover what had happened, as how it had happened; survey, not rescue, seemed the most compelling task.

Rescue, indeed, was out of the question. It was too late for anything like that. The interior of the church was ablaze with a festive brightness, gay festoons of flowers adorned the altar and chancel, and there was a warm, vital smell of burning wax and incense: entering from the severe, ubiquitous moonlight, it was like coming across a coloured illustration in a book after pages and pages of dull print, or like stepping right into the midst of a greetings card. Ruining, however, this overall effect of festivity was the long black mound of Condor's body, bereft of all its elegance, lying askew on the topmost step of the altar.

I drew closer and, conserving my same initial feeling of calm but abysmal defeat, saw that not only was he dead, but that he had been cruelly and systematically torn apart in the centre regions of his body. A surprisingly dark bloodstain had already reached the bottom altar step, and as I mounted the steps to approach the corpse I could feel the carpet squelch beneath my tread. His head, fringed by a now crimson collar, was intact, but lolled at an awkward angle to the rest of him, the face partially hidden by a fold of his cowl. His arms were flung wide and in his right hand he clutched a small, bright object – a silver cross – its crossbar rust-coloured and bent so far back as to resemble the tip of an arrow.

161

In his vicinity, the smell of flowers and incense receded before a stronger claimant. I did not look long: it seemed wrong and above all indelicate to have caught him thus in such a totally unguarded posture, he whose every image afforded to the outside world had been calculated for its effect down to the minutest detail. Besides which, flanking and overriding any such considerations, I could tell from the taste of saliva at the back of my mouth that I was very shortly going to vomit. As I made for the fresh air, I saw the second protagonist of this grisly drama crouched by the altar-rail, her hands tied to it by the improvised rope of a nun's girdle, the velvet bag firmly in place once more. It was the last I ever saw of her, and the last I thought of her for a long while: a small, crouching figure, bound and hooded like a hawk after the kill – sated, bloodstained and repulsive. I had from my first awareness of disaster, although for different reasons, already sponged her from my consciousness, and there, erased, obliterated she was to stay. The wound she had inflicted on me went deeper than the loss of her – her death or torture at the hands of Condor would have been nothing compared to this. No, the loss was manifold and total – never again to take her in my arms, never again to penetrate through her medium into a changed and brighter world; no more hopes, nor dreams nor projects: the future I had so looked forward to sharing with her, our brief past I had so relished, collapsed together into the narrow dimension of an intolerable present from which she must perforce be excluded if I were to survive. I could hold no more place for her in my mind.

I was sick into the roses – many times, I think. Some while later, looking down at my hands with bland curiosity as if they had been those of another, I noticed that they were deeply studded with thorns, but whether I had thus punctured them when trying to reach the window earlier, or while pressing myself in misery against the wall of the church, where I stood unnoticed and largely unnoticing for a long while after, I could not recall. I clenched them tightly, but to my dismay could feel no pain.

People – two, maybe three – talking in subdued undertones, bustled past me into the building and then out again, carrying mops, pails and bundles. It seemed like wartime all over again – the same confused acceptance, the same quiet, efficient tackling of the aftermaths of wreckage. At one point I heard the sturdy voice of Frogface instructing Sister Zoë, 'Get a needle, then, and some thread, for goodness' sake!' and then calling out impatiently to someone else, 'and ring the Bishop *first*, before we call the police. Don't panic, *think*!'

No one seemed aware of my presence. In the end it was Jitters who prised me away from the wall, but he had other things to do besides look after me and he left me there alone again, rocking feebly backwards and forwards on my unsteady legs. Dragging and swishing noises were still coming from the church. I flailed around uncertainly, wanting more than anything to achieve oblivion from the whole happening, or, failing this, distance from it. I wanted to be rid of it all. Like a sleepwalker or a drunk, or a half-anaesthetised patient trying to escape from the operating theatre before his turn is due, I began to grope my way towards the house. Once there, although I remember nothing about it, some vestige of resolution must have returned to me, for not long afterwards I had managed to pack my few belongings and was bicycling mechanically through the night, aware of little else but the hectic pedalling of my legs and the bitter taste of nausea in my mouth.

163

The books I had left behind in my haste were forwarded to my college two weeks later, together with a cheque for my services. There was no accompanying note, nor did I receive, then or later, any further communication from the Convent. And that in a way was the end of it. With the passing of time – and I mean, of course, the passing of years, of decades – the thought would sometimes come to me that the whole episode had been no more than a dream, a nightmare; or else that certain parts of it had. The boundaries between real and unreal, between factual and imaginary which I had used to keep so trenchant in my arsenal of methodological tools, refused to give or bend or bulge and accommodate, but I learnt to live with my memories after a fashion by the complex expedient of burying and blotting. I neither forgot nor remembered, that is. I shelved. I became in the end a philosopher of a sort, although not of the sort or the calibre that I should have wished: those few commentators I attracted described me as a positivist. I achieved outwardly a quiet, decorous and not unpleasant way of life – not such an unhappy ending after all, you may think – but I carried within me the while a festering, untouchable sore which proved in the long run as detrimental to my work as to my well-being; for, after all, what contribution to positivism can be made by a thinker who has known and loved a werewolf? Or, if this question is ill-framed, then what serenity can be found by a man who has loved a psychopath and who has deserted her for ever in her direst moment of need? And the fact was that I had done at least one of these things (I would no longer be prepared to add 'at most one') and, worse still, had never had the courage to decide which. I had bolted. I had run. I had turned my back on the past and sealed off a portion of my mind. I had committed the most heinous philosophical sin: dishonesty, and the gravest human one: cowardice. I had doubly failed – failed as a philosopher and as a man.

7

Towards dawn I fell asleep, but I was awakened what seemed to me only very shortly after by the arrival of two minibuses, which disgorged a group of noisy and enthusiastic participants in the coming celebration, or whatever it was the nun had referred to as the 'big do', on the lawn beneath my window.

This was doubly irritating, for besides sleep I should have liked – or, if liked is too positive a verb in this context, then certainly wanted or needed – to have been able to wind up my reluctant journey into the past by spending the morning revisiting in unhampered solitude some of the places where key events had taken place: not the other turret; not, definitely not, the church; but I felt that I could willingly manage a visit to the library now, or the boat-house maybe, if it were still standing. What I felt, in short, was a deep urge or longing just to wander around a little on my own and set a seal on my anamnesis.

The suppressed questions which had so tormented me on my arrival were no longer present: mere remembering had been sufficient to erase them, or to show me anyway their pointlessness. For it was there of course that I had gone wrong from the very start: I had asked the wrong kind of questions and had looked for the wrong kind of answers. Even Condor had been guilty in the end of the same mistake: Martina had not wanted to be exorcised or to be shown reality in the naked surface of a mirror; she had wanted a hiding-place, a refuge; she had wanted shelter. No, there was nothing to be gained at this late stage by investigation or by questioning; no point in looking for clues, in grubbing around in search of facts, in riffling through the books in the library to see if I could find tufts of long-forgotten wolf-hair between the pages. There was no further evidence to be examined, nothing more to be found out that could throw light on an episode destined by its very nature to darkness. The terminus of my journey, I now realised with a painful sinking of the heart, was not discovery of any kind but recognition of failure, and this being so, I had most thoroughly reached it. All I could hope for now was just to expose myself a little further, to lay a finger on the place where the sore had been festering all these years and find nothing but unfeeling scar tissue. I needed a confirmation of finality, really; nothing else but this.

With all the hustle and bustle that was going on, however, it did not look as if I were to be granted any such opportunity. Never mind, I thought resignedly, levering myself from the bed and beginning to dress; I had achieved enough. I had opened up the cupboard and remembered. Martina was dead and I was still alive, and neither of these facts, whether taken singly or strung causally together, seemed quite as depressing to me as they had before.

'Martina,' I said aloud, 'Martina. Martina.' There you are, I could say her name. I shut my eyes and concentrated, as I had never dared until now, on the image of her face, and it came before me instantly and clearly in a characteristic pose of hers: the burnished, sharp little head tilted to one side, breath suspended and mouth a fraction open as she listened in eagerness to something of interest that was being said. Yes, I could remember her now without effort and without anguish. The image retreated, and I could feel her portrait slipping back gently into the storehouse of my memory to occupy a new, slightly inflamed but unproblematic slot there, whence it could be called back at will or remain dormant, undisturbed.

Heavily tired and aching, but with a sense of well-earned release, I began the preparations for my departure. There was no sense in prolonging my visit – no sense even in speaking with the dwarf nun. I remembered her too now. She had been dressed differently then, not in the black and white robes of the fully fledged members of the order, but in the grey habit of the lay-sisters. Perhaps class-consciousness had made itself felt here too, and she had been granted a tardy promotion, or perhaps the hierarchy itself had been dismantled. I definitely remembered her now: minute and grey and in the background. It might well be that her tasks had included dusting the library, for that would have accounted for the undusted upper shelves, which would have remained, even with the help of the ladder, out of her stunted reach. A midget with a duster, what could she tell me that I wanted to know? Nothing now. Nothing at all.

While waiting for the taxi to arrive, I took a last short walk towards the only spot which offered seclusion from the overall atmosphere of pending jamboree. A tent was being rigged up on the front lawn and several side-booths were already standing, complete with tawdry drapery and still tawdrier occupants. As I made my way across I wondered intolerantly what occasion all these drab-looking adults could be celebrating to make them so vociferous and skittish.

168

'You can't be leaving *now!*' one bespectacled female had wailed at me on seeing my luggage, and another was now trying doggedly to pin some card or other on my lapel. Brushing her wordlessly aside, I crossed the lawn as nimbly as I could and made for the promising quiet of the cemetery, reflecting that it was indeed time I departed. Despite the fact that its population had noticeably increased in the interval, Frogface's favourite reading place was as deserted and quiet as I had hoped to find it. It was not hard either for me to find what all along I suppose a part of me had been looking for and another trying to ignore, for in the corner opposite that which extended its hospitality to the young airman – the close friend of Martina's whose end I had never, and I think rightly, wanted to investigate – two more dark-red marble stones stood out amongst the grey ones, similarly conspicuous for their colour and their inscriptions. Not wordy inscriptions. The first read: 'M.W. September 9th, 1930 – April 18th, 1949', and the second slightly smaller headstone beside it: 'H.W. April 18th, 1949 – April 18th, 1949'. Terse indeed, but for all their brevity revealing enough.

I heard the arrival of the taxi in the distance, but found it difficult to walk away from where I was standing; and when I did move it was not my feet that did so, but my knees, which crumpled beneath me and brought me abruptly face-down on top of the two small humps.

Was this shock or mere clumsiness? It is hard to say. It was I think not so much that the information transmitted to me in these two short but telling messages (and for the storing of which I had, alas, no ready pigeon-holes), really caused me further surprise or dismay – that Martina was long dead had struck me soon after re-entering the Convent, and that she had borne me a child should likewise have struck me as highly probable, seeing that I had expended so much personal effort towards attaining that very objective – but that she had died so young and so dramatically, and that the child, the brilliant and beautiful child I had dreamt of our fashioning together, had lived not even the space of one day, these were details that I would, if I had had the option, have gone to great lengths to ignore.

How long I would have stayed there like that, buckled uncomfortably over their graves with my nose pressed to the grass, I do not know, although I suspect that the thought of the taxi-meter clocking up its fare in English pounds of which I had none too abundant a supply would have brought me shortly to my feet and senses again; but I was soon aroused by a thin voice coming from somewhere very close to ear level: 'Your glasses, Ludwig,' it said. And raising my head from the damp of the grass, a few blades of it sticking unimpressively to my chin and forehead, I saw the dwarf nun again, standing close beside Martina's tombstone, which was high enough to shadow her almost entirely. 'Your glasses,' she repeated shyly, handing them over to me after having given them a rub with her apron. 'You haven't hurt yourself, I hope?'

I pushed the glasses back into place and began laboriously to strive for an upright posture once more; then, aware of the distance it would put between us when, strangely enough, I found the little creature so close to me of a sudden and was pleased that she should be so, I thought better of it and stayed kneeling instead.

The nun was looking at me fixedly with an expression of pity on her delicately crinkled face. I wondered if she had seen me fall, and wondered too how much she knew about past events, and about myself and the part that I had played in them. The wizened yet curiously youthful face seemed, seen thus level and close to, both penetrating and knowledgeable. Her words too when the shyness receded had about them a ring of informed intimacy, as if she knew not only a great deal, but knew too in advance the questions that must be going through my mind and wished to spare us both the embarrassment of my asking them.

'The H was for Hope,' she said simply, 'it was Sister Lucy who chose the name. Martina was too far gone by then to care.'

'Terrible it was, two young lives ending like that,' she added, shaking her head gently from side to side. 'I wasn't here when it happened, of course; we none of us were; it was when the typhoid scare was on and the whole place had to be evacuated. We were sent to our other Convent in Bournemouth – the whole community. Sister Lucy stayed on to help with the confinement; just she and Father Hugh – he stayed on too through it all. They did everything they could, the two of them, but they couldn't manage to save Martina or the baby. They did manage to keep things very quiet, though, and so I suppose in a way the typhoid scare was a blessing, as no one came near the place for weeks. When the news came through to us in Bournemouth, we had mass said for their two poor young souls. It was a terrible business, it was indeed.'

As the nun spoke, and although her manner of telling betrayed nothing other than a candid and moving sincerity, in my mind I began busily furnishing a translation of her words into a very different and very disquieting idiom; and while she was unfolding her blameless story of Martina's prolonged and difficult labour, of the unavoidable delay there had been in obtaining medical assistance, of the stillborn child and its posthumous baptism at the hands of Jitters, of his and Frogface's efforts to save the mother, and so forth, my translation

171

went its silent way, accompanied by images so vivid that it seemed to me the little nun could not help but see them too and partake in my unspoken commentary and its sinister lateral pageant.

Thus when she told me of the typhoid scare I could see Frogface sitting in her cubby-hole like a powerful spider in the centre of its web, engineering from there the entire preliminary manoeuvre in order to be left alone with Martina at the crucial moment of her labour; when she told me of Martina's death and the delivery of the child, I could see an equally resolute Frogface dispatching with compassionate efficiency two silver bullets of her own making (for this of course, had Condor only known it, is the standard way of securing permanent riddance from werewolves; and this is what a silver cross is needed for – they must be shot with solid silver bullets obtained from a molten crucifix), and covering up as she had done on the night of Constantine's slaughter the regrettably messy side-effects which such dabblings in the heroic inevitably produce. I could see her aiming, firing, and then rolling back her sleeves and cleaning things up, smoothing things over for the undertakers and rehearsing a tired and terrified Jitters in the story they were to provide for the doctor when he arrived. I could see it all as clearly as if it were being enacted in front of my eyes.

'Did the doctor get there in the end?' I asked mechanically, already guessing what the answer would be.

The nun looked at me hard, cocking her head on one side and clicking her tongue. 'I'm not sure of that,' she replied in a slow staccato; 'I seem to remember Sister Lucy saying that by the time he did it was much too late to be of any good. I suppose all he was able to do was just to ascertain their deaths and sign the certificates. She and Father Hugh had to manage nearly everything on their own. They did do all they could, you know, Ludwig; you

172

can rest assured of that. Sister Lucy was a trained nurse too, you know, and she had had a lot of experience during the war – I don't think a doctor's presence would have made much difference. Martina didn't suffer, but I don't think she put up much of a fight either; perhaps after all that had happened she didn't really want to go on living. She went out very quietly – like a snuffed candle, Father said, although he never liked talking much about it afterwards.'

So Martina had not suffered. Not officially, that is; not physically. Nor had she, although she was supremely equipped to do so, put up a fight. How much though, I wondered, had she fought and suffered during the lonely months of her pregnancy? Had she been afraid? Had she sought help? Had she too foreseen the possible mechanics of Frogface's final solution and realised that neither she nor her child were destined for survival? And had this in reality been the end that she herself had desired and courted?

The nun went steadily on with her tale, while the gory pantomime danced on between us, losing in vividness and plausibility only when it reached the point of the elimination of the child: here, try as I might, I could no longer fit Jitters into the picture. I could just imagine him refusing aid to Martina; I could see him turning aside and praying for her death; I could even see him closing his eyes and stopping his ears as an armed Frogface bent over the bedside and dealt Martina a well-aimed *coup de grâce*; all these possibilities I could conjure up in my mind's eye, but when it came to downright infanticide, and to the Jitters I had known and liked taking part, however passively, in the perpetration of such a cold-blooded and terrible crime, my imagination faltered, the picture froze to a standstill, and all I could see was his puzzled and kindly face looking out at me as if to ask,

173

'Now why should I go and do a thing like that, Wig, for goodness' sake?' No, I thought wearily to myself, I was granting my imagination too free a rein; the nun's narrative might well fall short of the truth, but things had not gone as I had portrayed them either – not quite like that, surely.

'Poor little Martina, poor little Hope,' she was saying. 'We have mentioned both their names in our Intentions every day since, but there's no one left now except myself who knows who they were, so I expect when the Lord calls me too they will be dropped. Ah, well.'

With this she finished her telling, but taking advantage of the strange bond which had managed to unite us till now on a plane far removed from the verbal and which was still unbroken, I said quite naturally, although never for a moment taking my eyes off hers, 'They didn't harm the baby, did they?'

She looked at me with an intense sadness, then answered softly in the same natural tone, 'No, of course they didn't, Ludwig. Of course they didn't. They never harmed the baby.' Then she looked away: the moment of exposure was over, and her voice wobbled as she corrected herself hurriedly by adding, 'The baby was dead already: stillborn. I thought I made that clear.'

'You made everything clear,' I said, staring straight at her, refusing to be drawn back again so swiftly within the bounds of conventional communication. 'She's still alive somewhere, isn't she? Tell me if she is. Don't you think I have a right to know?'

'If you had any right, you forfeited it a long time ago,' the nun answered quietly with no trace of censure. Then she turned her head away from me abruptly, and with that the thread of unveiled and unspoken communication, if indeed it had existed anywhere outside my own imagination, was broken.

174

I got creakily to my feet and bowed my head in silence. We stood there for some seconds longer, then I took her hand in mine and made a formal and final goodbye.

'Goodbye it is, Ludwig,' she replied in quite a different tone, withdrawing her hand and neatly decapitating a daisy with the toe of her shoe. 'Before you go, perhaps a little offering towards the Convent would be in order. We don't usually make a charge for overnight accommodation, but we do rely on our guests to show their appreciation in the way they see fit.'

'Of course, of course,' I said hurriedly, 'how very remiss of me.' I fumbled for my wallet, trying unsuccessfully to think of a sum which would leave me with a maximum of both decorum and funds; and it was, in contrast to the nostalgic leave-taking that I had prefigured, with this awkward exchange of crumpled notes pressed into the midget's palm that my dealings with the Convent came to their definitive end.

Almost definitive, that is. For as the taxi drew away from the house, my imagination – particularly active that day, and in this instance abetted by my fickle eyesight – played one last cruel trick on me; and looking back at the turret where I had caught my very first glimpse of Martina, I saw as clearly as if she had been no mirage but a real person in the solidity of flesh, bone and blood, a young woman standing there framed by the open window, looking wistfully out into the distance – white-faced, dark-eyed, and with a great blaze of untameable red hair: an apparition which, I can assure you, did nothing to counteract my sense of utter failure.